BLOOD MONTH

To Barbara,

Happy birthday!

David.

William Vaughan

BLOOD MONTH

William Vaughan

y Lolfa

To E.C.A.P

First impression: 2013

© William Vaughan & Y Lolfa Cyf., 2013

Cover illustration: Suzanne Carpenter

ISBN: 978 1 84771 656 9

FSC

Published and printed in Wales
on paper from well maintained forests by
Y Lolfa Cyf., Talybont, Ceredigion SY24 5HE
e-mail ylolfa@ylolfa.com
website www.ylolfa.com
tel 01970 832 304
fax 832 782

1

Michaelmas Term, 1971
14th November

Llanover Grange's chapel was full for the Remembrance Day service in which those who had died in two world wars were honoured. A marble scroll listed the former masters and boys who had risked and lost all in the abattoir of battle. Poppies were everywhere; in buttonholes and scarlet wreaths which would later be laid beneath those now faceless names.

In the knowledge that she would not witness this scene again, Rhian Evans saturated herself in the solemn atmosphere. She stared at the altar, with its gilded candlesticks, and wondered how many tears had been shed by her predecessors as they had watched their pupils prepare for war. Thank God, there was no conflict to tear David away.

In spite of everything, Rhian still recalled with gratitude that glittering morning when their eyes had first met. Just two months ago, as stems of sunlight poked through these same lancet windows, she had seen a pupil whose profile exerted an immediate fascination. From the moment he had turned his head and looked at her, Rhian had been captivated.

He was in the fifth form ranks, so nearly sixteen, and slender. An olive bloom to his skin contrasted with the black of his blazer and tie. Straight blond hair hung neatly from a side parting. His eyes were a copper-sulphate blue and there was a hint of gold above his upper lip. The young teacher had admired youths of this sort before, but never one who combined such a range of attributes. He looked even more enticing in an emerald jersey and white shorts when she had chanced to see him loping along the wing in a hockey match, his thighs long and sensually smooth.

It was idle to regret David's existence, as futile as cursing a rainy day. The youth had bewitched her. Fate had pitchforked her into a love that many saw as tainted, but there was nothing she could do other than accept it. Come what may, she would ignore the Headmaster's command and proceed with their afternoon rendezvous.

The richly carved choir stalls and cold white walls engendered an aura of calm which was comforting and an opportunity for putting her emotions into some sort of perspective. Ahead, Christ hung on a cross of gold. Would that gentle figure, dangling from those cruel nails, condemn her? How had she violated the basic tenet, 'Do to others as you would have them do to you'? Her feelings for David had harmed nobody. In fact, such response as they had evoked suggested that they might even be welcome. Yet she knew the Reverend Griffiths' appalled reaction was the Biblical one. As the

Headmaster was never late, Rhian wondered why his stall was still empty. Ernest Davies, a less than skilful organist, had practised 'O Valiant Hearts' so many times that he was note-perfect.

Dr Harrold, the Deputy Headmaster, kept glancing at his watch and whispering to his wife, Margaret, who was looking deathly. Perhaps the rumours of marital problems were true. He left his stall and approached Rhian. A beery odour wafted from his mouth as he said, 'Miss Evans, would you try to find our beloved leader for me? He might be unwell, I suppose. I'll instruct the Chaplain to commence the service in five minutes whether he's here or not.'

Indignation inflamed Rhian's face as she hurried from the chapel. Being sent on a schoolboy errand was not to her liking. As she swept past the Housemaster, Arthur Thomas raised a pair of shaggy eyebrows and smirked.

The Headmaster's house, a 1960s box painted a lurid shade of pink, appeared lifeless. A Sunday newspaper poked, like an insolent tongue, from the letter-box. Rhian's hammering drew no response so she ventured into the garden from where she was able to peer through the kitchen window. There was no sign of breakfast debris, not even an upturned cup on the draining board. Perhaps the Headmaster was in his study. Reluctantly, Rhian marched towards the school.

Her BA gown, which she wore to chapel only

because she had been ordered to do so, billowed and flapped behind her like a pennant. Chippings crunching underfoot, she hurried up the drive but, as she approached the main entrance, the strains of 'Crimond' drifted through the autumn air. They had started without her. She stopped to catch her breath and decided against slipping into chapel for what remained of the service. Instead, she would return to Saint Teilo's, the boarding-house where she was the Assistant Housemistress, for a cup of tea.

The most direct route involved crossing the hockey pitches and passing the old stable block which had been converted into changing rooms. As she strode along, she noticed that one of its double-doors was open and the porch light was shining. In the euphoria of yesterday's triumph over Monmouth School, such mundane matters had evidently been neglected.

Rhian's innate decency overcame the inclination to turn a blind eye so she made the detour necessary to remedy the situation. When she looked into the porch in search of the light-switch, she heard the hiss of running water. The Games staff had not even bothered to turn off the showers. She made a mental note to have a word with Mr Wood.

The teacher stepped into the changing-room to discover that the floor had been transformed into a shallow lake, littered with islands of soggy shirts and shorts. The water was not deep enough to require the removal of her fashionably long boots so she paddled across to the tiled area which was veined with cracks. Staying upright on the slippery surface, while evading the spray, tested her sense of balance.

As she reached for the stopcock, she noticed a figure face-down in the water! Frantically, she twisted the metal wheel until the cascade ceased. A man's head almost filled the drainage trough, creating a partial blockage which accounted for the flooding. Rhian tugged at the saturated jacket and trousers until his head came clear of the gutter and the water began to gurgle away. With an unceremonious heave, she turned the body and encountered her first close-up of death. Rigor mortis was complete. The corpse was rigid. The wan face had a peculiar blue tinge to it. There was a swelling to the left temple and a frothiness about the lips. Rhian stared at the shocking sight, and a hot, bitter nausea rose up in her throat. She touched one of the bleached, wrinkled hands. It was enough. She began to run. Apart from a short – but vital – detour, she did not stop until she reached the chapel steps.

She was standing in a puddle of water, formed from the dripping hem of her gown, when the act of worship ended. Dr Harrold emerged through the arched door, closely followed by his wife. Both were startled by Rhian's appearance.

'What on earth's the matter, Miss Evans? What's happened to you?' asked Dr Harrold.

'It's the Headmaster,' she answered. 'He's dead.'

'Dead? Are you sure?' the Deputy Headmaster demanded. 'Have you rung for an ambulance?'

'He doesn't need medical attention. I think you'd better phone the police.'

2

14th November

A black Rover scrunched to a halt on the gravel in front of a pair of doors which stood below an ornately carved porch. Detective Sergeant Jack Jones stared over its steering wheel at the Victorian Gothic mansion, once the home of a coal-owning family and muttered, 'I wonder how many miners died to pay for this place. Must cost a small fortune to send your kids 'ere. And what for? I'd close the lot of 'em!'

Detective Chief Inspector Tom Llewellyn slid out of the car, stretched his arms and paused to admire the gabled stone facade. A breeze rustled a cold greeting through the avenue of birches which lined the drive. 'You can't deny it's handsome, Jack. I wish I'd brought my sketchpad.'

Jones, who was well over six feet tall, slammed the driver's door eloquently.

As he strode through the grounds of Llanover Grange, Tom Llewellyn did not look nor sound out of place. A stranger could easily have mistaken him for one of the masters. Apart from the odd strand of silver, his neatly brushed hair and clipped moustache were the colour of iron filings. His jacket and trousers were shades of grey, though a splash of warmth was provided by a maroon tie. By no means small, he was dwarfed by his sergeant, but he carried his rank effortlessly, thanks to a Celtic charm and cunning which he could conceal when occasion demanded.

After more than two decades in the force, the sight of mutilated bodies lying in pools of gore still upset Llewellyn, so he was relieved to discover that this victim displayed remarkably few signs of violence. 'All the preliminaries have been taken care of, I presume,' he said quietly.

'Yes, sir. Photographs and fingerprints have been taken. His pockets 'ave been searched and a wallet, containing £25 in notes and a credit card, was found. Dr Meredith is on 'is way to examine him and do the postmortem.'

'Good. We need to know how he died before we can proceed sensibly but, assuming his death wasn't accidental and that we can rule out robbery as a motive, we come back to the old adage that most people who are murdered know their killer. Was he married?'

'No, he seems to 'ave been a confirmed bachelor, as they say,' Jones replied, in a cynical tone.

'Petty jealousies flourish in places like this,' said Llewellyn. 'My gut instinct tells me we won't have to look beyond the school grounds for our killer. Interview every member of the teaching and domestic staff, and see to it that all the boys who've been on the premises this weekend give statements. By the time we're done, Jack, we'll have stared the culprit in the eye. You mark my words.'

Llewellyn breathed heavily as he knelt to inspect the late Headmaster's head. 'Well, he hasn't been battered to death, that's for sure. In fact, he's the cleanest corpse I've ever come across.'

'Because he was found with the showers still running, sir. One of the teachers – a Miss Evans – discovered 'im, face down in the drain about eleven this morning. These showers were full of lads at four o'clock yesterday afternoon, so he must've been killed between those times,' Jones explained.

'Unless,' Llewellyn mused, 'he was killed elsewhere and brought here afterwards. But that's unlikely. From the swelling on his temple and the bruising under his left eye, I'd say someone has smacked him hard across the face. The damage to the back of his head might mean he fell backwards or was given a second blow. Forensics will tell us exactly how he died, but my guess is that he drowned.'

Jones' forehead furrowed. 'How do you make that out?'

'The slight frothiness about his lips suggests asphyxia so there'll be water in his lungs. What's more significant is that anyone angry enough to use the proverbial blunt instrument usually bashes the victim's brains out. There's blood all over the place. But this chap was hit once, maybe twice. Our killer seems to have been in control of his emotions. The attack began violently, but ended clinically. Why bother to drag him in here if it wasn't to finish him off? I suspect that the Headmaster was held down in the water to drown.'

'Maybe the killer switched on the showers to wash away any incriminating evidence,' Jones suggested. 'They've done a damned good job of it. There are some old cricket bats over in the corner, sir. Do you think he could've been 'it with one of those?'

'In the heat of the moment, people pick up the nearest thing to hand so it's possible, but our man, if he's as calm and calculating as it appears, won't have tossed his weapon back into that pile for us to find. Have them examined but tell the uniforms to keep searching. Anything suspicious is to be bagged.

'Right, it's time to have a word with the lady who discovered the body. I think I'll interview her in the staffroom. We're not likely to disturb any evidence there. Meanwhile, have a good look through the Headmaster's house for me, Jack. We've all got a skeleton or two in our closets, even clergymen.'

'Especially clergymen,' Jones muttered.

3

14th November

The staffroom was poky and shabby. A single window permitted the entry of some gloomy daylight. Fixed to one wall was a board covered in yellowing notices. Tattered gowns hung from a line of hooks and there were several tiers of pigeonholes. Scattered over an oval table were dog-eared exercise books. The armchairs looked tired and the settee's springs sagged. It seemed to Tom Llewellyn a dowdy, downtrodden room suitable only for dowdy, downtrodden people. He could not imagine his colleagues on the force tolerating such conditions for a month, much less a lifetime.

A timid knock announced an arrival at the door.

'Come in,' he called and a pale, pretty woman, whose long dark hair dangled onto her shoulders from a central parting, entered. As he gestured for her to sit on the opposite side of the table, Llewellyn wondered how someone so young could possibly be a teacher.

'Miss Evans, I assume. And what do you teach?'

'History,' came the shortest of replies.

'Ah, a fascinating subject… Now then, how long have you been at Llanover Grange?'

'Since September. This is my first term.' Rhian saw no

reason to add that, twenty-four hours earlier, she had been told that it was also to be her last. The Headmaster's death might prove timely.

'Do you like it here?'

'It's exhausting because the hours are so long.'

'But a teacher's lot can't be too bad in a place like this.'

Rhian nodded but volunteered nothing further.

'I gather you discovered the Headmaster's body soon after eleven o'clock this morning. What were you doing in the changing rooms at that time?'

'Well, I'd missed the morning service because Dr Harrold – he's the Deputy Head – sent me to look for the Headmaster. I tried his house but couldn't find him. Then I heard singing coming from the chapel and I assumed our paths had crossed.'

'So why didn't you go back in?'

Rhian's feet shuffled with embarrassment. 'To be honest, I was annoyed that they'd started without me. Anyway, I'm not a believer, so I thought I'd nip back to my room for a cup of tea instead. I was taking a short cut across the playing fields when I saw the pavilion door wide open and the porch light on. I went over and found the place awash. As I was turning off the showers, I noticed a man sprawled in the water. I turned his body to see if there was anything I could do, but he was cold as marble. When I touched his hand…' Rhian paused and stared down at the table, 'I just started to run.'

For a few uncomfortable moments, Llewellyn thought she might burst into tears so he assured her, 'If it's any consolation, Miss Evans, there was nothing you could've done. The Headmaster had been dead for hours by then.'

'Oh, I knew that,' Rhian said. 'If there'd been any doubt, I'd have called for an ambulance. Perhaps I should have rung for the police. Why I returned to the chapel steps and stood there, like a statue, I don't know. My gown was sodden and I could've caught my death of cold. It was the shock, I suppose. I've never seen a corpse before. When Dr Harrold came out, I told him what'd happened and he took charge. His wife invited me into their flat and gave me a cup of sweet tea to settle my nerves.'

'Was the Headmaster popular? How did you get on with him?'

So far, Rhian had been pleasantly surprised by the blandness of the detective's questions but, from this point on, she knew she would have to lie.

She stared ahead, recalling the events of the previous afternoon, and realised that they might well be construed as a motive for murder. She would say nothing about them. She would say nothing about being summoned to the Headmaster's study to be acquainted with the contents of a jilted lover's letter. She would say nothing about Gareth's revelations concerning her sexual behaviour which had caused the Headmaster to demand her resignation. She would say nothing because it was possible that no other living person knew of yesterday's trauma. And that was how she intended things to remain.

The Reverend Griffiths had promised to veil her impending departure in secrecy until the end of term, but had unwisely added that he had not yet confirmed her dismissal with the Chairman of Governors. So that morning, as her gown flapped against her shivering legs, Rhian had removed the incriminating letter. Its malicious allegations could slip into the grave alongside the Headmaster. Gareth's revenge, which had been perched conveniently on top of the Headmaster's in-tray, was now nestling inside her blouse pocket.

At last, the teacher answered Llewellyn's questions. 'We rarely spoke. He was an old-fashioned disciplinarian so, no, I don't think he was popular. He was a private man, the sort it's hard to chat to but, if anyone knew him, it was Miss Morris, his secretary.'

Llewellyn's dark eyebrows arched. 'Go on.'

'There was gossip that Miss Morris was in love with the Headmaster, and had hopes of marriage. He was less guarded with her than most of the teaching staff, though I doubt if he felt the same way.'

'Have you heard rumours of anyone with a grudge against him? People in authority make enemies.'

'Newcomers like me don't know people's real feelings,' Rhian replied.

'I appreciate that,' the detective interrupted, 'but even what seems like tittle-tattle might be helpful.'

'The only people who were openly critical were Dr Harrold and Arthur Thomas, but it'd be ludicrous to think that either of them would be involved in murder.'

'Murder? So you don't think the Headmaster's death could've been an accident?'

When Rhian laughed at the absurdity of the question, Llewellyn noticed that she had a fine set of even, white teeth. 'No, I don't. Why would a fully-clothed man wander into the boys' showers while they were running? Anyway, there was damage to the front and back of his head.'

'The postmortem should reveal how he died but it does seem suspicious,' Llewellyn agreed. 'You mentioned two members of staff who made no secret of disliking the Headmaster. Let's start with his deputy.'

'Well, Dr Harrold expected to be appointed to the Headship when the position became vacant a couple of years ago. The governors' choice of the Reverend Griffiths came as a shock and, since then, he's hit the bottle. You can smell alcohol on his breath even before lunch, and his drinking is said to be putting a strain on his marriage.'

'In other words, he's an alcoholic,' Llewellyn suggested.

'Oh, I'm not saying that!' Rhian protested. 'Ask

Arthur Thomas – he's the Housemaster – because he's known Dr Harrold a lot longer than I have.'

'I'll do that. Tell me about Mr Thomas. Why did he fall out with the Headmaster?'

'Arthur used to be Head of Games but, nowadays, only teaches a few lessons of Maths on top of his boarding house duties. The Headmaster thought his teaching load was too light, and would've preferred a graduate as Housemaster. He's been trying to persuade Arthur to pack his bags for months.'

The detective grinned. 'Wouldn't most teachers have leapt at such an offer?'

'Probably, but Arthur knows he's got a cushy number here. He's served the school for more than thirty years and thinks he's entitled to a full pension.'

'As a motive for murder, being offered early retirement doesn't rank too highly,' Llewellyn said dismissively. 'By the way, where were you between four o'clock yesterday afternoon and, say, nine in the evening?'

'I was in my room most of the time,' Rhian replied, after a momentary pause. 'As I was on duty, I had tea with the boarders and then popped in and out to keep an eye on them.'

'Does that mean you were alone for long periods between those times?'

'I suppose so,' she agreed reluctantly, unnerved to realise that she was regarded as a possible suspect.

Before the detective could continue, there came a

thump on the door and a bald pate poked around its edge. 'Can I 'ave a word with you, sir?' Jones asked.

'All right. I'd just about finished.'

Rhian was keen to take her cue. 'May I go?'

'Yes, but please don't leave the premises until you've made a statement to one of my officers.'

With a sigh of relief, Rhian closed the door. She glanced at her watch. Past two o'clock, the appointed hour of her meeting with David in Llanover. Her solemn promise to be present lay in pieces and there was nothing she could do about it. She returned to her room and wept.

4

4th September

Rhian was determined to find out more about the Adonis. Perhaps his talents and hobbies might offer an opportunity of meeting, but discretion was vital. Too much interest in a pupil she did not teach might arouse suspicion among her colleagues. Miss Janet Morris, the Headmaster's secretary, seemed a safer source of information.

'Oh, that must be David Wyn-Williams,' she told Rhian confidently. 'He's the only boy in the fifth form who could fit your description. Most of the others seem to be sporting crops of acne at present, but David's a lovely-looking lad. He's one of our better behaved boys and rather charming, but not as intellectual as his father who's a lecturer, I believe. He takes after his mother. She's a bit of a stunner too. On parents' evenings, you can hear the men drooling over her.'

'He does stand out from the herd,' Rhian agreed, trying to sound matter-of-fact but, like a sheet of blotting paper, she was absorbing every word. Each snippet about the youth and his family fascinated her. To judge from his lithe figure, there was a chance they might share an enthusiasm for sport but, for once, Janet Morris was uncertain.

'I'm not sure about his sporting talents, dear. You'll have to ask Mr Wood. I do know he's a talented actor. He's bound to get a leading part in the end-of-term production of Julius Caesar.'

Rhian was heartened by this last detail and wondered whether the English department might welcome her assistance.

A few days later, Rhian cursed audibly when she saw her name on the roster which shot down her few 'free' periods. Then she realised that her name was pencilled against 5S, David's form. The day dribbled past until the bell for the last lesson hammered. 5S were due to have Chemistry in one of the ancient laboratories which she had never entered. This proved to be a cavern full of smeary test tubes, flat-topped acid bottles and pock-marked benches. The teacher's dais and desk were covered in a film of chalk dust.

The ailing Mr Watson had sent in a list of questions, so Rhian had no undue anxiety about her poor scientific skills. Her duty was to maintain law and order while the boys presented at least the semblance of working.

At last, David entered the room, gossiping with a friend. The class had not been forewarned of Mr Watson's absence and their surprise at being supervised by a stranger was obvious. As the last stools were occupied, Rhian hoped that silence would descend automatically, as it sometimes did with her younger pupils. But the chattering showed no sign of abating. She would have to assert her authority. She had not wanted this. Fifth formers were not easily cowed. For the first time, she regretted her eagerness to enter the profession straight from university, without any teacher training. She knew that first words weigh heavily in the classroom, but David's mere presence caused her voice to misbehave.

Speaking louder and more tremulously than normal, she began, 'Mr Watson has a cold which is why I'm here, but he's set you some questions from your textbook to prevent you getting bored. Please don't ask me for assistance as what I know about Chemistry can be written on the back of a stamp.'

Her honesty provoked some guffaws and a derisory whistle, so she turned her back and began to scribble the question numbers on the board.

'Shall I give out the books, Miss?' asked a voice.

'That would be helpful,' she said gratefully. Rhian glanced around to discover the speaker's identity and was astonished to find herself looking at David. 'I'll give you a hand as soon as I've finished,' she said, while thinking, what lovely, long eyelashes you've got!

Reluctantly, she turned her attention to the rest of the class.

'You'll find these questions on page 74. If you wish to work in pairs, I've no objection provided you do so quietly.'

Rhian scrawled the last numbers so that she could be near David for as long as possible. When she entered the stockroom and saw him bending over a pile of dog-eared books, a surge of lust swept over her. Suppressing the desire to throw her arms around his waist and then slide her tongue across his neck – the only flesh on view – was like some mediaeval penance.

Unaware of the emotions which he had released, David picked up the books and turned around. Rhian felt a guilty glow suffusing her face but she targeted her eyes upon the youth's and challenged them to linger. A smile parted his lips and rewarded her boldness. Her stomach lurched in a nauseous sort of relief. There were no elevated thoughts. In this uncomplicated, physical response, David's disquieting power over her was confirmed.

Together, they dispensed the books and then she thanked him.

'You're welcome,' he replied.

The pupils began their task. Despite some excessive noise, Rhian made a stab at marking exercise books, but her mind and hands were too unsteady. Even this brief encounter with the youth had destroyed her equilibrium.

5

7th September

'Is this the queue for A Level English?'

The voice was masculine but a trifle high-pitched. Rhian turned and was agreeably surprised to discover that its owner, with his long auburn hair and round-rimmed glasses, resembled John Lennon. Though not her type, he was almost handsome.

Her patience was already on the ebb. 'Yes and, at this rate, we're going to be here all night. Are you joining too?'

'That's the idea,' he said.

For some reason, Rhian decided to explain. 'I've never studied modern literature. At my school, D.H. Lawrence was still regarded as racy stuff. And I'd like to broaden my knowledge of Shakespeare as well.' She did not elaborate upon her motive for this. 'I'm new to the area,' she continued. 'I started teaching at Llanover Grange recently and I'm desperate for an excuse to escape into the real world. Tuesday's my half-day and this was the only subject on offer which I fancied... By the way, I'm Rhian.'

'Gareth. Aren't teachers supposed to spend all their

free time marking books and preparing lessons?' he asked, with a cynical laugh.

'Some do, believe it or not, but I think teachers are as entitled to a life as anyone else. This course is about meeting like-minded people, and studying something for its own sake. I've got all the qualifications I want, so I'm not going to take any examinations.'

'God, I wish I was in your position,' he muttered. 'I've got to improve my D to a B grade to get into university next year. I managed Bs in History and Economics so I don't need to retake those.'

'Couldn't you get in somewhere with those grades?'

'I'm only interested in York. My girlfriend'll be starting her second year there soon.'

'Oh, I see,' she empathised.

'Would you like a coffee?' he asked. 'If you'll keep my place, I'll get a couple. I'm gagging for a fag, but I'll have to settle for caffeine. White with sugar?'

'White without, please,' she said, tapping her stomach.

During his absence, Rhian decided that Gareth was probably three years younger than herself which accounted for her unusual ease with him. He was tall and leggy, and she liked his vaguely hippie aura. When he returned, she surprised herself by asking if, when they had registered, he would like something more potent to drink and was gratified when he said that he would.

The Conway was the nearest pub, a stone's throw from the college.

It was a smoky, charmless place with a youthful clientele. In a recess stood a jukebox blaring out 'Hey Jude' and a one-armed bandit in constant use. Rhian would have preferred to drive out to some timber-framed inn in the Vale of Glamorgan but it was clear that Gareth was not that sort.

*

After only a couple of lessons and pub visits together, Gareth arrived on Saint Teilo's doorstep. Visitors rarely used the front door and Rhian, who had soon discovered that Arthur Thomas' deafness was acute when anyone rang the bell, opened it. At this hour, a guest was still acceptable. She was surprised when he bent forward to kiss her and snaked out his tongue, but she allowed it into her mouth and liked its taste.

'Let's go up to my room, away from prying eyes,' she advised. 'Are you all right?'

'Mair went off to university today.'

'So you're feeling lonely.'

'To put it mildly. You're stuck out here in the sticks with a bunch of kids. I thought you might like some company too. You don't mind, do you?'

'No... but I'm on duty. There's no way Arthur'll swop

with me now, but you're welcome to stay for a drink and a chat. Only white wine, I'm afraid.'

As they entered the long bed-sitting room, he pulled her to him and whispered, 'What I really need right now is for you to hold me.' Then he rubbed a cold hand around her neck and the other across her breasts. He was urgent, almost rough. As his cobra-like tongue jabbed again and again, Rhian realised what Gareth wanted. For the first time in her life, she considered – once she had dealt with the boys – submitting to her sexual urges.

*

A small leaf caught in a strand of cobweb hanging from the lattice window. Through a shaft of sunlight which slipped between her incompletely drawn curtains, Rhian watched the leaf struggle to break its silver chain. The failure of the wind to end its captivity irritated her, and she felt curiously impelled to intervene. She jumped up and moved, as quietly as the uneven floorboards would permit, to the window which squeaked open, allowing a chilly draught to engulf her. It was irrational to endure discomfort to free a dead leaf but it gave her a peculiar satisfaction.

She returned to bed trying not to intrude her cooling body into Gareth's warmth. She lifted the sheets to admire him. Until last night, she had never touched a naked man. Now she recalled, with a certain contentment, the sensation of her nipples firming in his mouth and her moans as he had sucked. Their thirsty bodies had drunk deeply of each other but, when she remembered how she had been visualising David as she climaxed, a clammy sweat broke upon her skin.

Gareth's even breathing gave way to semiconscious stirrings. 'What's the time?' he asked.

'Nearly seven o'clock. The boys have a lie-in on Sundays but I'll have to smuggle you out of here soon.'

'Have you really never slept with a man before?'

'No, you've had the privilege of deflowering me. These days, I don't suppose many women preserve their virginity for twenty-one years. To be honest, I'm glad to be rid of it.'

'Well, you can make up for lost time with me any time you like,' he offered. Then he rolled onto her and lifted himself into the missionary position. Rhian gasped and grabbed and groaned while he struck repeatedly. Once he fell aside, swallowing mouthfuls of air, they were both as damp and limp as facecloths.

'God, that was good,' he said. 'You don't perform like a novice.'

Their banter was disrupted by vigorous thumping on the door. Rhian glanced anxiously at her watch. 'Arthur's never this early at the weekend. Go and get dressed! Heaven help us if anyone sees you.'

She shoved Gareth, who was clutching a bundle of his clothes, into the bathroom while she snatched her dressing gown. When she opened the door, a smirking pupil revealed nothing more urgent than a reminder from Mr Thomas that she was due to supervise the boarders at breakfast.

'Yes, Phillips, I was well aware of the fact. Kindly leave the door on its hinges next time. I'll be down shortly.'

Rhian got the uneasy impression that the boy was staring over her shoulder and, when she looked for what it might be, she saw Gareth's white Y-fronts lying on the pale blue carpet.

6

13th October

Dr Harrold was a dapper man, a little over forty years of age, who had spent the bulk of his career at Llanover Grange despite an aversion to all things Welsh. A competent administrator, he had risen effortlessly through the ranks of the English department to the position of Deputy Headmaster, and had taken it for granted that he would succeed to the Headship upon the retirement of Harold Davies two years earlier. The unexpected appointment of the Chaplain of an evangelical school in Swansea had left the old Harrovian distraught. From the moment the governors' decision was announced, Dr Harrold had felt a hostility towards the Reverend John Griffiths that had festered into contempt. An iciness was almost tangible when the two men were in the same room.

One of Dr Harrold's annual chores was arranging the school's Careers' Evening. He had detailed Rhian to supervise a band of boarders in providing visitors with a cheap sherry at the start of the event. A variety of local businessmen had presented themselves to impart advice, and also to attract potential recruits. Rhian gazed around the hall and felt a little sorry for the boys who had parents in tow. Everyone seemed vaguely afraid that they might somehow disgrace themselves.

Her spirits were beginning to dip when she heard the Headmaster boom, 'Good evening Mr and Mrs Wyn-Williams, how nice to see you! Ah, and David, I hope you'll find the occasion useful, though you'll be with us for some time yet, of course.'

Mr Wyn-Williams, who was tall and well-proportioned but unremarkable except for a drooping moustache of the kind popular in the Sixties, said, 'Actually, David has suggested transferring to the Further Education College in Llanover to do his A levels. Your sixth form fees are considerable, so we've no choice but to take the idea seriously. We'd like him to stay but, to be blunt, we can't afford it.'

Griffiths shot his pupil an angry glare as he replied, 'I think you'd regret taking David away from us. He's settled here and very popular. Continuity in education is vital and your son will benefit enormously from being taught in small classes by our experienced staff. As for your dilemma, I quite understand, but you mustn't worry yourselves on that score. Bursaries are available in deserving cases, and I can assure you that one will be allocated to David next September. I'll write to you with the details.'

'Well, you've taken my breath away, Headmaster! I didn't come here tonight with the intention of holding out a begging bowl, but that's a very generous offer, isn't it, darling?'

David's opinion was not sought. He appeared to be grimacing, but his mother, a beautiful woman with lustrous blonde hair and sapphire eyes, was beaming and nodding in agreement. Rhian's face was split by a banana-shaped grin. To overhear news which would keep David at the school until he was eighteen was a delightful surprise. Suddenly, the Headmaster had soared in her estimation. But it troubled her to see the sadness in the youth's eyes.

*

The scent of sherry was on Dr Harrold's breath when he returned to Saint Illtyd's, the senior boarding house, where he and his wife lived in a cramped but self-contained flat.

'I'm home, dear,' he called.

Mrs Harrold was several years older than her husband. She had once taken a pride in her dark good looks but, in recent times, had become careless, almost shabby. Her lustreless hair, which was frosted with grey, straggled over her ears and forehead. She sat, twisting a handkerchief in her hands, and was clearly distressed. There was an unhealthy gleam in her eyes.

'What's the matter, dear? You look upset.'

'How very perceptive,' she remarked.

Dr Harrold tried to put a comforting hand on his wife's shoulder, but she brushed it away. 'Don't touch me!

I can smell the alcohol on you from here. You promised that you wouldn't touch another drop of the stuff.'

'I had no choice in the matter. Having a glass of sherry with the parents is part of the job. Even Griffiths had one and he's virtually teetotal.'

'I suppose he managed to stop after one glass. How many did you have?' she snorted.

'A couple, that's all,' her husband lied. 'It was insipid stuff, but I needed something to sustain me through an evening in that ridiculous man's company. Would you believe he was going round the hall doling out bursaries in a pathetic attempt to keep pupil numbers up?'

'Don't change the subject, Derek. I can't take any more.'

Dr Harrold sighed. 'There's no need to be melodramatic, dear. What a fuss over a few sips of sherry!'

An angry pink swept the pallor from Mrs Harrold's face. 'This isn't about a few sips of sherry! Unless you admit that you've got a problem, we're finished. I'm not prepared to put up with it any longer.'

'What red-blooded man doesn't like a drink?' Dr Harrold snapped.

'But you're drowning yourself in whisky, Derek! For God's sake, go to the doctor or visit Alcoholics' Anonymous. You must do something!'

'Oh, don't be hysterical, dear. All I need right now is something to eat and a good night's sleep.' He glanced at the empty decanters on the rosewood side-table. 'Where's the whisky and gin?'

'I emptied the lot down the sink while you were out. For your own good.'

Dr Harrold's lips began to quiver. He hesitated and then raised his hand. 'You stupid bitch!' he yelled, as he slapped his wife hard across the face.

'That's the end,' she sobbed. 'I want a divorce.'

7

21st October

Rhian's offer to assist with the school play had been spurned but, as a female, Dr Harrold considered her suitably qualified to help with the costumes. She had not realised how fateful the fitting might prove until, late one afternoon, Matron barked, 'Those who need togas, strip to your underclothes!'

The boarders were used to Matron wandering in and out of the dormitories unannounced, and proceeded to reduce themselves to school vest, pants and socks. Day boys, like David, were more bashful about undressing in public, particularly as most of them chose not to wear vests. Slowly, all of the aspiring senators removed their school uniforms.

David's lithe, lean body was much as Rhian had imagined. Nothing in his physique was a disappointment. In fact, the layer of flesh and muscle which covered his torso was almost too close to the perfection of a Greek statue, though his olive colouring meant there was no deathly pallor to it. Perhaps his thighs were more muscular than she remembered from the hockey match.

The baggy bedsheets insisted upon slipping from shoulder blades causing much amusement. For a while,

Rhian watched Matron and Miss Morris pulling and pinning the costumes into place. She decided to lend a hand by tugging and inexpertly attaching a few pins to Edward Phillips' toga. Having established her innocence of purpose, she turned her attention to David. Somehow she resisted the temptation to run her fingers down the parallel lines of fine hair which gilded either side of his neck.

'Turn around and let me have a look at you,' she suggested and, as if he were a mannequin, Rhian instinctively placed her hands on his shoulders to aid the pivoting process. Her left landed safely on cotton, but her right alighted on flesh. A shudder of gratification rippled through her and a guilty glow suffused her face. She felt light-headed, almost faint, with pleasure. It would not do to pass out here, so she retreated. 'I think it needs Matron's touch,' she explained lamely.

Once there was no bodily contact, Rhian was able to stare into those hypnotic eyes and wonder how much kindness lay behind their sky-blue sheen. She was aware that a turquoise ocean, basking in brilliant sunshine, can be icy just below the surface.

8

22nd October

A surreptitious glance at the 5S register had enabled Rhian to discover David's address. Instead of leaving for the half-term break directly after lunch, she determined to snatch one more glimpse of his face. Ten days without sight of it was too much to bear.

Denuded of its occupants, Saint Teilo's seemed sad, almost sepulchral. Rhian packed her case before she set out for the market town of Llanover. She intended to take an afternoon stroll along Heol Don and, if she happened to encounter any of the occupants of number 46, it would appear by chance.

The house proved to be a detached dwelling which faced Llanover's only park. She decided to sit on one of the wooden benches and keep watch on the red-brick building with its eminently Victorian sash windows. After a period of fruitless observation, Rhian retreated to the rear of the house where the daily living quarters were likely to be situated. Here, she discovered a cinder-shod lane at the end of the garden. A set of iron railings, overgrown with privet bushes and reinforced with a row of conifers, provided cover. The lane gave the impression of being little used and Rhian decided that it would be safe to linger.

French windows overlooked the lawn and through them, causing a surge in her heartbeat, she saw David lounging in an armchair lit by a cosy, table-lamp glow. For half an hour or more, she watched and waited until, at last, the youth rose to his feet and stretched his arms, allowing his admirer to see that he was dressed in a check shirt and jeans. He spoke to someone out of her line of vision and disappeared.

Daylight had departed and the air had cooled uncomfortably but, just as she was about to end her vigil, a light appeared in one of the upstairs windows. Posters on the bedroom wall suggested she might be able to steal another sighting of David so Rhian postponed her departure again.

The youth strolled across the room, presenting his handsome profile and rewarding her patience. Several times, he sauntered to and fro. Suddenly, he stopped to peer down the garden. Rhian drew back, afraid that her presence might be detected, but David resumed his meanderings. She sighed and told herself that she was unlikely to be spotted in the darkness when masked by a screen of foliage.

Luck chose to be generous that evening. When David reappeared, he was clad only in the jeans and was cleaning his teeth. Rhian had never envied a toothbrush before. Even at this distance, his semi-nakedness magnetised her eyes. Then the youth was briefly framed in the window as he jerked the curtains together. The show was over.

Peeping Tom had been blinded. Even if modern punishments were less vicious, Rhian realised that she was playing a dangerous game. But there was a compulsion driving her that would not be denied. Come what may, she would return tomorrow and see more.

The following afternoon, she spent several hours in the park and the streets of Llanover in search of David. The autumn sky wore a slate-grey scowl but, unlike its neighbours, there were no cheerful lights inside number 46. Clearly, the Wyn-Williams family was not at home, but Rhian refused to depart without seeing the youth. She would wait, if it meant staying till midnight.

It was, in fact, nearly nine o'clock when headlights swung into the alley, bathing it in a ghostly glare. Rhian realised that the beams were about to swamp her and she would be discovered. In desperation, she shoved herself into the privet hedge so hard that its slender branches scraped and scratched her neck. The low railings stabbed her back and she swore silently.

When the car braked short of the house, a wonderful wave of relief washed over her. The sounds of slamming doors and babbling voices were music in her ears. As the voices grew more distinct, the car's engine revved and the headlights looped into a garage. Rhian merged into the darkness and, with a renewal of hope, heard the garden gate groan and the noise of chattering fade. Lights illuminated room after room. There was another groan and Mr Wyn-Williams followed his wife and son homeward.

Rhian stared at the outline of the house and waited for a light to appear in David's bedroom. At last, the boy's invisible hand flicked the switch and, once more, no effort was made to draw the curtains. His stalker ditched all sense of shame and scruple and gazed longingly at him, employing the concentration of some seedy private eye.

Without warning, David appeared at the window and began to peer in her direction. Rhian had the uneasy sensation that she had become the object of attention. David even pressed his nose against the window pane to get a closer look. When he drew back, she wondered what – other than her presence – could have attracted such scrutiny?

As the inky leaves rustled in a restless breeze, the youth returned to the window and began to remove his shirt. He showed no eagerness to replace it with a pyjama top nor to move out of the spotlight. Was he deliberately exhibiting himself? His manner encouraged Rhian to indulge her most erotic fantasies. Smiling into the dark, the motionless god stood there, his arms crossed. Suddenly, they pushed upwards, making his body into a full-length Y-shape as he tugged the curtains, drawing a shroud over Rhian's desires.

Back in the boarding house, the realisation dawned that David, in spite of appearances, might object to her behaviour. If he complained to his parents, awkward questions were bound to follow. There was nothing to do except hope he would not betray her. For most of that night, sleep refused to release her from a troubled conscience.

All next morning, Rhian waited anxiously for the telephone to ring, but not a word about her whereabouts the previous evening was spoken. By teatime, she was convinced her worries were unfounded. Earlier, Janet Morris had popped in to inform her that she was not permitted to spend the entire holiday on the school premises helping herself to free electricity and gas. Her third visit to Heol Don would have to be the final one, at least for now.

When she arrived, David was already in his bedroom. He kept moving to and from the window as if he were keeping watch for her! A smile – seemingly of recognition – lit up his face, and he began to strip to the waist revealing his sculpture-like torso. When he assumed a position at the window which allowed her to see that he was now naked, save for a pair of Y-fronts, the impact was almost ecstatic. The youth thrust his hands behind his head, extending his chest so that the ribs and taut stomach muscles were countable. She could see the circles of his nipples and envisaged using her tongue to raise them into a pair of peaks. As her imagination ran riot, David smiled into the darkness again, and Rhian dared to believe that he was seeking her approval for this striptease.

Suddenly, Mr Wyn-Williams entered the room. Like some moustachioed villain from a silent film, he wagged a finger at his son and drew the curtains. Time passed, and it became clear that the performance had ended.

Unwillingly, Rhian turned to head for Saint Teilo's but, after a few steps, noticed the light above the back door come on. A silhouetted figure emerged from the kitchen. David, now clad in a jumper and jeans, strolled nonchalantly down the lawn to within a few yards of his votary. He stood there, hands in his pockets, for several minutes, flicking the occasional glance in the teacher's direction. Not a syllable was uttered but Rhian was convinced that he was aware of her presence. Some sort of masque was being enacted, but what it signified, if anything, was beyond her comprehension.

The next morning, Rhian set off for her parents' home in Cardiff. No matter what the consequences, she had decided that, one day, she would tell David everything she had seen and felt.

9

5th November

Gareth had drained a bottle of claret while he read and reread Mair's letter. He had struggled to grasp the finality of its content, but there was no mistaking the indifference of its tone.

Once more, he perused the neat writing on the blue paper which he had torn, with all the excitement of a child ripping into birthday cards, from its envelope just a few hours earlier. Perhaps the words had mystically rearranged themselves into a more welcome message.

Dear Gareth,

Thanks for your letter and sorry for the delay in replying.

I'm afraid it won't be possible for you to come and stay with me next month as I've already invited Paul Sutton – a third-year Geography student – to be my partner at the Xmas disco.

You won't believe this, but we're getting engaged next summer! Paul is gorgeous! And clever! If he gets an upper-second, he'll be able to stay on to do an MA and we'll be able to share a flat while I finish my degree. He's got a great sense of humour and I know you'd like him.

Must close now as we're off to the pub!
Love,
Mair xxx

Breaking out of something like a trance, Gareth had telephoned the office where he worked as a temporary clerical assistant, to say he was unwell. The rest of the day had been a mist of moping. Announcing her proposed engagement in such an offhand manner was unbelievably thoughtless. Surely she should realise that he would forever hate the name Paul?

The clock radio flicked to four o'clock. The wine had made him maudlin. He flopped across the bed and grimaced at his reflection in the dressing table mirror. He recalled admiring Mair's long, sunburnt legs from this same position and tried to ignore the image of them straddling his successor. In the couple of months since those afternoons of sex together, a chasm had opened of which he had been completely unaware. Now she was with someone else. How long would that last? He was well rid of her, he rationalised. Rather than wallow in this trough of self-pity, he decided to seek solace with Rhian. She did not stir his deepest passions, but her pert body was only a little less attractive than Mair's and would serve as an antidepressant.

At that moment, weary after a day in the classroom, Rhian sat and stared into the twilight. She was listening to Simon and Garfunkel's 'Sounds of Silence' and contemplating whether her relationship with Gareth had a future. It was several weeks since their last encounter. With a wry smile, she recalled how they had bathed together and used the bathroom mirrors to stoke their ardour. If those slivers of glass could talk, they would tell a tale to send the gossips' tongues into overdrive. But their separation over half-term had not troubled her.

After her belated sexual baptism, she had sometimes visualised Gareth's hirsute body and been frustrated by the lack of physical communion. This was sheer lust. She did not miss his companionship. Thoughts of him rarely entered her head while, by contrast, David's absence nagged like an impacted wisdom tooth. Just to set eyes upon him again had provided the instant relief of an extraction.

Rhian did not care that these emotions were widely considered unacceptable. David would soon be sixteen and entitled by law to marry and father children. He was not a pre-pubescent child without a mind of his own. But Rhian also knew, if she were to declare her feelings, that she would jeopardise her career and, if she were to act upon them, might risk imprisonment. Of course, her desires must remain in the realm of fantasy.

She rose to switch off the record deck when a series of crashes came from the front door. Before she twisted the key in its lock, she had guessed that Gareth would be responsible. 'Didn't I tell you to 'phone before coming here?' she asked coldly. 'You won't be able to stay long because it's the boarders' fireworks display later.'

'But I need to see you.'

'Tea is in twenty minutes and I'm on duty,' she muttered, making no attempt to hide her exasperation.

Gareth felt queasy. Too much wine and too much emotion, and now this hostile reception. Rhian had once seemed so timid but, nowadays, she was abrupt, almost aggressive.

They adjourned to the sanctuary of her bed-sitting room. 'What's the matter?'

'It's Mair. She's getting engaged to some bloke called Paul next year and they intend living together.'

'Oh, I see. Is she serious? I thought she wasn't much older than you.'

'So what? The point is we spent last summer planning to be at university together and sharing a flat. And now she's discarded me like a used condom.'

'Out of sight, out of mind,' Rhian commented, too tartly for Gareth's liking. 'Nothing I say will make any difference to the way you're feeling. Words of consolation always sound trite and trivial.'

'Well, don't say anything!' he snapped. 'I just can't face being alone tonight.'

'I should be in the dining hall,' she replied evasively. 'There's probably a riot going on right now without me. Stay for a while. Make yourself a coffee, if you like. Why don't you come to watch the fireworks? It might take your mind off things. I'll be back as soon as I can.'

When she left the room, a surge of nausea welled up in Gareth's stomach. He rushed into the bathroom where the bulk of his vomit hit the toilet bowl. Only a small, sordid mess splashed onto the linoleum. He slid down and propped his back against the wall, feeling temporary relief. He did not move in case there were lesser waves to come. A sallow face stared back from the mirrors around the bath. He had never been so wretched in his life.

*

As a girl, Rhian had loved bonfire night and, though there was something of that air of anticlimax which adulthood brings to such festivities, she was enjoying its sights and sounds and smells. Another highlight of November, her birthday, was only days away. She was a true Scorpio, passionate but secretive. It pleased her that she would no longer have to celebrate the event as a virgin.

She felt rather smug, parading about with a good-looking, if wan, young man, but this sensation evaporated with David's unexpected arrival. A number of day-boys had returned to school to take advantage of the free fun on offer. She watched David make his way to the edge of a group of giggling boarders who were inebriated by nothing more potent than each other's company and some bottles of very weak shandy. When he began speaking to Edward Phillips, Rhian saw her chance.

Whether they wanted her or not, she would join them. This was the opportunity she had been craving.

'Hello, it's David, isn't it?' she asked unimaginatively.

The youth turned his head, allowing a close-up of a profile that was etched into her memory.

'Yes, that's right.'

'And what do you think of our display?'

'Not bad.'

Rhian continued, 'Mr Thomas got a good deal by buying the fireworks at the last moment. He seems in his element setting them off. I'm in charge of crowd control.'

'As usual,' Phillips muttered, followed by a long swig of shandy.

'Now, now, Edward,' she said, but the rebuke came with a conspiratorial wink.

'Do you like it here, Miss Evans?'

Discovering that David not only knew her name, but was also prepared to take the initiative to sustain their conversation, pleased her enormously. 'The hours are long, but it has its compensations,' she replied. 'The Vale is a beautiful part of Wales, and I've made some new friends, Mr Lewis for example.' She nodded at Gareth, but he did not reciprocate.

'Nobody calls me Mr Lewis,' he whined. 'My name's Gareth.' He felt excluded from their teacher-pupil chat and considered it had gone on long enough. 'I've not eaten a thing all day, but I think I could manage something now.' He tugged on Rhian's arm and tried to head for the smoky barbecue.

'Hang on!' she protested, unwilling to be literally dragged from such a promising situation. 'Would you like anything, David?'

'I'll have a hot dog. No onions, please,' he answered, accompanied by a grateful smile.

As they moved away, Gareth snorted, 'Why the hell did you do that? I came here to be with you, not a bunch of school kids. Give him his hot dog and tell him to sod off.'

'Being with kids is what I'm paid for,' Rhian retorted. 'You chose to come here. Nobody twisted your arm. Anyway, what do you want?'

'Nothing! I've lost my bloody appetite. Just get something for the pretty boy,' he sneered.

'Keep your voice down! The Head's about and I don't want to attract his attention. It'll only take me a moment to give this to David. Why not have some chips? They look OK.'

'I'm not hungry,' he intoned.

Rhian hurried to complete her errand and was helped by the fact that David had detached himself from his peers and met her half way. Not for the first time, he looked at her so intently that she felt her knees tremble. 'One hot dog without onions. I'm afraid Mr Lewis has stomach trouble so I'll have to go.'

'Miss, I need to talk to you,' the pupil said, suddenly urgent. 'Away from this place. Could we meet at the weekend?'

Rhian's heart skidded through several beats. Surely, David must be able to hear its uneven pounding? She should, but would not, ignore such a request. 'Have you anywhere in mind?'

'The old bandstand in the park opposite my home. You know where it is. About two o'clock on Sunday afternoon? It's important, Miss.'

His pleading tone made a refusal impossible. 'Of course I'll come…' Then she remembered. 'Damn, I'm on duty this weekend. Will it keep till the following Sunday?'

Though he looked crestfallen, David replied, 'Yes, but you won't forget?'

'No, I'll be there. Promise,' Rhian assured him, in the certain knowledge that there would be little else on her mind for the next nine days.

*

The last flickering flames of the bonfire guttered as Rhian and Gareth returned to her room.

'I thought those fireworks would never end,' he moaned. 'Can we go to bed now?'

'Not tonight. You're going to be the main topic of

conversation in the school tomorrow. The Head was staring at us all evening, and I can't afford to take any liberties with him. Arthur might not worry about what we get up to in bed, but Griffiths is a different matter. He doesn't approve of sex outside marriage and, if he found out about us, it would cost me my job. You're hopeless at getting up early and it's difficult enough to smuggle you out of here at the weekends when everyone has a lie-in. We'll have to be more careful from now on.'

'If you don't want me to stay, come straight out with it!' he demanded.

Her patience snapped. 'All right. I don't want you tonight.' She paused and then added, 'Or any other night.'

The certainty in her voice took his breath away. After several seconds, he hissed, 'You bitch! If I went out and killed myself, you really wouldn't give a toss, would you?'

Rhian gave a hollow laugh. His selfishness and egotism were as much a part of him as his sight and hearing. 'Oh, for God's sake, don't drag threats of suicide into this! You're not the only person who wants someone who doesn't give a damn. It's a fact of life. Get used to it. You'll survive without me – and without Mair – because you've no bloody choice in the matter.'

Gareth glared at her, his mouth agape. 'Perhaps you'd prefer to spend the night with your pretty boy? You spent most of the time chatting him up. I couldn't get a word in.'

This unexpected accusation caused Rhian's face to flame with embarrassment. 'Don't be so ridiculous!' she lied. 'He's just a kid with a problem, and I agreed to meet him so we can discuss it.

'Deny it all you like, but I know there's something going on. You never look at me that way!'

Rhian tried to think of a clever retort but failed, so she shouted, 'Shut your evil mouth!'

He grinned. 'Ah, the truth hurts.'

Anger almost caused her to lose control of her tongue, but a sense of self-preservation prevailed. 'David's handsome, but that doesn't mean I want to have sex with him. Unlike you, I can control my libido.'

'Oh, I know,' he sneered. Before slamming the door, he added, 'That's why it'll be another twenty years before your next lay!'

10

13th November

Rhian's birthday dawned a misty and mournful grey. Her eyes were underlined in blue indicating that she had not slept well. She ploughed through Saturday morning lessons until Miss Morris delivered a memo from the Headmaster requiring her for interview at two o'clock. The unexpected note ruined her appetite. Instead of the dining room, she headed for the Headmaster's garden which was one of the few places out of bounds to boys and so conducive to meditation.

The Headmaster was not the sort to interrupt a free afternoon for a routine chat. This summons must be significant. Perhaps there had been a complaint about her teaching methods which were liberal by the school's standards. Far worse was the possibility that David's parents had discovered news of their planned meeting.

In spite of a wind, her palms were oily. The tension in her neck was causing her head to ache, so she adjourned to the main vestibule a full twenty minutes early. Too nervous to sit, she began to pace about, throwing cursory glances at some prints of Welsh castles. The sound of a raised voice came from the Headmaster's study. Rhian edged closer and heard Miss Morris' distinctive tones.

'We're not getting any younger, John. You promised me that we'd announce our engagement at Christmas...'

'I promised no such thing!' the Reverend Griffiths interrupted. 'A betrothal was your suggestion, Janet. I agreed to consider the idea, and I've done so. It's true that I miss the companionship which marriage would bring, but I'm too set in my ways, too fond of my independence. If you think about it, we'd be together twenty-four hours a day! How many marriages would work under those circumstances? We've both forgotten how to consider anyone's feelings but our own. The chances are we'd make fools of ourselves.'

'So what?' she demanded. 'They say it's better to have loved and lost, than never loved at all. I understand that you're frightened of commitment, John. Of course we'd be taking a risk. Everyone who marries does that. There are no guarantees in any relationship, but I'm sick of being the butt of staffroom jokes from the likes of Christine Draycott. I don't want to die an old maid!'

'My decision is final. A cleric has to weigh the pros and cons of marriage more than most. If we were to prove incompatible, a divorce would cause a scandal in a place such as this. I'm sorry, Janet, but there will be no engagement.'

Her hopes and desires obliterated, Miss Morris surrendered to a deluge of tears. They were coursing down her furrowed face when she swept past Rhian. For almost the first time in her career, she was less than the perfect secretary. At two o'clock precisely, Rhian's white knuckles rapped against the study door.

'Come in,' the Headmaster called, his voice betraying no sign of disturbed emotions. Rhian remained standing while the Reverend Griffiths, ensconced behind a leather-topped desk, perused a handwritten letter.

Rhian's eyes conducted a sweep of the room. It was unchanged since her only previous visit on the day of her interview. There were the same undistinguished portraits of former Headmasters, the same dusty book-lined shelves and the same oppressive atmosphere. She was on tenterhooks because she was convinced that Griffiths was reading a complaint.

At length, her superior looked up and asked, 'Now then, Miss Evans, what can you tell me about this Gareth Lewis?'

'Not a lot,' she answered perfunctorily, though she was taken aback by the mention of his name. 'We both attend an evening class at the F.E. college in Llanover. On Tuesdays, my half-day,' she added.

'Enlighten me as to how well-acquainted you are with him.'

'We've met a few times socially, for a drink,' she lied with surprising ease.

'Is that all?'

'He was my guest on bonfire night. You may have seen him with me.'

'Oh, so that was Mr Lewis. He's younger than I

expected.' The Headmaster fingered his smoothly shaven chin and then waved the piece of paper in the air. 'I've received a letter from him which contains some disquieting allegations about you. Even if such charges had been made anonymously, I wouldn't have been able to ignore them but, as he's provided his name and address, he expects a reply so I'm duty bound to enquire carefully into the matter.'

Rhian licked her dry lips and retorted, 'I hardly know him so he's in no position to make a complaint about me.'

'Then I'll be direct. Mr Lewis claims to have been your lover. He has provided a list of the dates when he slept in your bed. Of course, I'm prepared to listen to your version of events, but it would be very difficult for me to believe that all these details are the figment of a fevered imagination.'

The clergyman's comments caused the blood to gush from Rhian's face. She recalled Edward Phillips catching sight of Gareth's underpants in her room, something which he would not have kept to himself and evidence which would probably be discovered, if any investigation was launched. There seemed little point in denying the affair. Perhaps honesty might save her.

'We spent a few nights together,' she confessed. 'But when I refused to let him stay on bonfire night, we had a blazing row. That letter must be his way of gaining revenge. I never dreamt he could be so spiteful. Our relationship was very brief and is clearly at an end. I can assure you that I'll never do anything so indiscreet again.'

'So you admit that you've been having sex with a young man who is little more than an acquaintance?'

Rhian squirmed and nodded.

'And intercourse took place in your room in the boarding house when you were supposed to be on duty?'

'Yes,' she muttered miserably.

There was a lull as the Headmaster laid the letter on his desk. 'Now, Miss Evans, we come to another issue raised by Mr Lewis.'

Rhian felt her stomach churn in disbelief. If it had not been empty, she would have covered the tasteful Chinese rug in vomit. Surely Gareth had done enough mischief already?

'He also suggests that you harbour sexual feelings for one of our pupils.'

Rhian struggled to marshal her thoughts. 'As one of the causes of the quarrel was my talking to David Wyn-Williams, I assume he's the pupil in question.'

'A "blond boy called David" is mentioned in the letter,' the Headmaster confirmed. A smug smirk creased his face.

'Well, I've never said nor done anything improper to any pupil,' she declared. 'David approached me and asked my advice on a personal matter, and he suggested a venue and time for meeting. As I'm a newcomer and female, perhaps he thought I fitted the bill as a counsellor better than one of the masters. My interest in him is purely professional. Ask him yourself.'

The Reverend Griffiths was taken aback by the vehemence of her denial. 'Has this meeting with Wyn-Williams taken place?'

'Not yet.'

'Then you must cancel it. Mr Lewis is adamant that you confessed to being attracted to the boy.'

'That's a lie! Gareth was the one who kept referring to David as "the pretty boy", not me. I simply said he was handsome which is a statement of fact. There's nothing sinister about it. I'm sure even you'd agree with it.'

The Headmaster was bemused by this observation. 'That is neither here nor there,' he responded tetchily. 'Any sort of comment upon the attractiveness of a pupil to an outsider is unwise.'

'Well, I'm not ashamed of anything I've said to David. We've only spoken on a couple of occasions.'

The Headmaster was not convinced. 'I've done my best to be sympathetic, Miss Evans, but Mr Lewis' letter is damning. That you could embark upon a relationship with this young man so casually is appalling. To invite him into your bed, when you should have been supervising the boarders, beggars belief! I cannot tolerate such misconduct by a member of my staff. It's clear to me that you're unfit to hold the responsibilities that come with a residential position. I doubt if you're suited to the teaching profession at all. You're fortunate not to be dismissed out of hand but, as I'm sure we both wish to avoid a scandal, I shall permit you to stay with us until Christmas. Then you will leave quietly so that your reputation – and that of the school – will remain intact.'

Rhian stood in silence, like some miscreant pupil, as the torrent of innuendo cascaded over her.

'I'll be put to the inconvenience of acquiring a replacement at short notice but that can't be avoided. Fortunately, History teachers are ten-a-penny. Of course, I won't be able to provide you with a reference. My advice, Miss Evans, is to go into employment where temptations of the flesh are restricted to adult company. Though you seem competent in the classroom, you're the sort of woman who can cause grave moral damage in a school.

'I'm confident that Commander Hopkin, the Chairman of Governors, will support my judgement so I would advise you against making an appeal. The fewer people who know the real reason for your departure, the better. On the last day of term, I propose to make an announcement that you are leaving to commence a career outside teaching. Don't inform anyone of this in advance, not even Mr Thomas. Your resignation will be on my desk on Monday morning. Is that clear?'

This was an outcome beyond Rhian's worst imaginings. She blinked at her superior uncertainly. 'Do I have a choice? I don't belong to a union so perhaps I should consult a solicitor before I put anything in writing.'

'Any solicitor worth his salt will advise you that, in these circumstances, you're being treated leniently. My principal responsibility is to the school, and the truth is, Miss Evans, it would be a dereliction of my duty as Headmaster if I were to allow you to remain here.' When Rhian closed the door upon her interrogation, she felt as if she had been released from the pillory rather than granted an indulgence. Her eyes began to brim with tears forcing her to rush for the staff toilet where they overflowed in a silver stream of misery.

Her world lay in rubble. One malicious letter had brought it crashing down. How she had underestimated Gareth! She had never suspected such Machiavellian depths. Now, like a midge entangled in gossamer, she could see no escape. Griffiths had been so ready to believe his every word rather than hers. The problem was that his bloody letter was true! She did find David attractive, to the point of obsession. Goaded by some probing lawyer, she would probably admit it. And what if David was dragged into an enquiry? He might reveal the voyeuristic nature of her visits to his home. Rhian blanched at the thought. Her cause was hopeless. Ignominious though it was, she would accept the Headmaster's terms. With one exception. Tomorrow's liaison with David would go ahead.

11

16th November

The strains of a Bach fugue ushered Rhian onto the chapel steps where she was taken aback to be greeted by the towering figure of Sergeant Jones.

'Excuse me, Miss, but my boss would like to 'ave a few words with you. He's at the station in Bridgend.'

'You don't mean right now, do you?' she asked incredulously. 'I'm teaching all morning.'

'Oh, you needn't worry about that. Dr Harrold 'as already agreed to sort out cover for your lessons. I'll drive you down there and arrange a lift back.'

As Jones accelerated out of the grounds of Llanover Grange, a sense of foreboding gripped Rhian which intensified with her first sight of the police station, a concrete and glass cuboid of the sort popular with architects and nobody else. If its design was intended to dispirit all who entered, it was a striking success.

After a long wait in a corridor tiled in a symmetrical green and white pattern, Tom Llewellyn invited her into the interview room. The detective's manner was graver than it had been on their previous encounter and his opening words confirmed Rhian's worst fears.

'It saddens me to say, Miss Evans, that the last time we met, you were less than straight with me.'

'I don't understand,' she muttered, but her instincts were screaming that Llewellyn had somehow got wind of Gareth's letter, despite the fact that she had stolen and later burnt it.

The policeman's confiding tone had evaporated. The hunt was afoot. 'Oh, I think you do. Let me make myself clear. Yesterday, I had a revealing chat with Commander Hopkin, the Chairman of Governors. He told me about a phone call he'd received from the Reverend Griffiths last Saturday afternoon which, according to forensic evidence, was just an hour or two before he was murdered. You were the subject of their conversation. Do you really expect me to believe you have no idea why that would be the case?'

Rhian still feigned puzzlement in the hope that a complete account of Gareth's letter had not been aired. 'Well, I'm not a mind-reader.'

Llewellyn continued, 'The Commander told me that the Headmaster had received a letter raising concerns about your sexual conduct. It was sent by a young man. Unfortunately, we don't know his name, but you should be able to help me on that point as he claimed to be your lover.'

'My private life is none of your business,' Rhian declared, a little desperately. 'Why don't you read the letter to find out?' she asked, in the certain knowledge that Llewellyn could do no such thing. When she saw discomfort register in his eyes, she decided to press home her advantage. 'I'd be interested to see it myself.'

The detective frowned as he was forced to admit, 'We don't actually have the letter. We've searched the Headmaster's house and study and your personal file but, so far, it hasn't turned up. Even if we don't find it, I'm confident we'll discover the identity of the man who sent it, but your unwillingness to assist me is noted. Let me tell you the gist of the letter as the Headmaster told it to Commander Hopkin...'

'But without it,' Rhian interrupted, 'aren't we in the realm of hearsay? So what's the point?'

Llewellyn puffed out his cheeks in exasperation and retorted, 'You are here because you've been accused of being unfit to remain in the teaching profession. The Headmaster terminated your employment on those grounds last Saturday afternoon. As well as your relations with this man, Commander Hopkin says you were accused of being besotted with one of your pupils. Will you tell me his name?'

Rhian tried to remain calm, but was struggling to catch her breath at this development. She snapped, 'It's rubbish!'

'You do realise, I assume, that teachers aren't allowed to indulge in physical contact with their charges?'

'Of course I do! I've never behaved improperly with any of my pupils...'

Surprised and irked by her defiance, Llewellyn silenced her with a wave of his hand. 'Right. Then let's go back to the letter in which all these allegations were made. Can you throw some light on its whereabouts?'

'No, I can't,' Rhian lied.

'Can you confirm that you were questioned about its contents and that, as a result, the Headmaster dismissed you?'

Commander Hopkin's baleful intervention, and Janet Morris' knowledge of their meeting, seemed to make further denial of these facts futile. Rhian admitted, 'Yes, but those allegations were a tissue of lies. I was intending to take advice about suing Gareth for defamation of character.'

Llewellyn seized on her first slip of the tongue. 'Ah, so we now have a clue as to the identity of the letter's author. Thanks for that. But, if you're as innocent as you claim, why does Commander Hopkin think you were prepared to accept the Headmaster's demand for your resignation?'

'He's wrong! That letter libelled me. I had no intention of leaving the school.' Rhian was astonished at the ease and conviction with which she delivered such untruths. If she repeated them often enough, she might even come to believe them herself.

'Why didn't you tell me anything about the letter and its consequences last Sunday? You're an intelligent woman. You must have realised that being fired for gross misconduct gave you a stronger motive for murdering the Headmaster than the likes of Dr Harrold and Mr Thomas.'

'As the accusations against me were false, and irrelevant to your enquiry, I saw no reason to inform you about them. Why should I? You were asking me about the Headmaster's murder, not about my personal life…'

Cynicism covered Llewellyn's face as he interrupted, 'But the two things are intimately connected. Let me put the sequence of events to you, and you'll see what I mean.

'One: the Headmaster receives a letter accusing you of sexual impropriety with a young man, and possibly a pupil.

'Two: the Headmaster interviews you, finds the charges proven to his satisfaction and dismisses you.

'Three: the Headmaster is murdered at a time when you don't have a worthwhile alibi.

'Four: you are the one who happens to stumble upon the body when you should have been in chapel.

'Five: the letter incriminating you mysteriously disappears.

'To be frank, Miss Evans, you've been downright deceitful in your dealings with me. It's impossible to tell when you're lying or not.'

Tom Llewellyn gazed into Rhian's bewildered, amber eyes and declared, 'You had the motive and opportunity to get rid of your troublesome superior, and I think you took your chance. It's clear to me, Miss Evans, that you murdered the Reverend Griffiths!'

12

17th November

'Songs of praises, songs of praises,

I will ever give to thee;

I will ever give to thee.'

Treble and breaking baritone voices intertwined to conjure that strangely ethereal sound which only adolescents can evoke. Ernie Davies thundered out the last chords of John Hughes' stirring tune and 'Guide me, O Thou Great Redeemer' brought the service to a climax.

Crow-like in his black gown, Dr Harrold strode to the lectern and began the ritual of announcements which he hoped would soon become his daily duty. 'The death of the Reverend Griffiths has made this a week of unprecedented sadness,' he intoned. 'And I'm afraid, I have more unwelcome news. As you may know from some lurid reports in the press, our late Headmaster did not die from natural causes. I regret having to report that Miss Evans is being detained by the police in order to assist with their enquiries.'

An outburst of whispering erupted which Dr Harrold quickly quelled. 'Be quiet! Remember where you are.

And let me remind you that every member of staff has been interviewed in the course of this investigation, as have some of you. I'm sure Miss Evans will be back in our midst shortly. Until then, a supply teacher will be engaged to take her lessons while Mr Thomas and I'll do our best to cover the duties in St Teilo's.

'Let me warn you all that I will take a dim view of rumour mongering. These are traumatic times, but we must try to get back to something like normality, which is why there will be lessons as usual today.'

Each mention of Miss Evans' name was like a punch in David Wyn-Williams' abdomen. The teacher was innocent. He knew this because he had killed the Reverend Griffiths! With a single blow from his hockey stick, he had shattered the Headmaster's skull.

Guilt was eating into David like maggots feasting on a putrid carcass. For days, sleep had rarely released him from a wretchedness so unbearable that he had even contemplated walking in front of a train. And now a blameless woman, and one who seemed peculiarly drawn to him, might be facing a murder charge in his place.

During morning break, he sought out Edward Phillips who, though younger and not a friend, he knew through a shared liking for hockey. Phillips was also a boarder in Saint Teilo's, and the possessor of an unusual independence of mind, so would know more about Miss Evans than most.

'Hi, Ed, how're you doing?'

Phillips completed a swig on a can of cola before replying, 'OK. You?'

'Not so good. It's this business about Miss Evans,' David said, in a classic of understatement.

'Why's that?' Phillips asked, with a quizzical hitch of his black eyebrows.

'Well, you know her better than me. You don't think she's capable of murder, do you?'

Phillips tilted his head and pretended to give the matter deep consideration before smiling and saying, 'Nah... but then I didn't take her for the type to have a bloke stay with her overnight either.'

This news made David's face look even more crestfallen. 'Are you sure about that?'

'Positive – unless Miss Evans has taken to wearing Y-fronts – but that's not for public consumption. As far as I'm concerned, she's a decent sort.'

'I think so too. That's why I wanted to talk to you. You see, I know she didn't have anything to do with the Head's death. But I need advice. Away from the flapping ears. Can I see you after school?'

Intrigued, Phillips agreed to this unusual request. 'Come to my dorm, and I'll see to it that we're not disturbed.'

In the short interval between lessons and the boarders' tea, David hurried to Saint Teilo's. In Phillips' dormitory, the furniture had been squeezed together to accommodate as many boys as possible but there was still only room for six beds. Phillips slept at the far end where he was already stretched out. Curiosity had made him uncharacteristically punctual.

David began, 'What I'm going to tell you is the gospel truth. Will you swear to keep it to yourself?'

Phillips elbowed himself upright and his face assumed a sincere frown. 'All right. Now just get on with it.'

David hesitated, having second thoughts about treating a fellow pupil as a confessor, but then plunged headlong. 'The reason I know Miss Evans had nothing to do with the murder is that I did it.'

The whites of Edward Phillips' eyes widened. 'Say that again!' he gasped.

'I killed the bastard. I smashed him across the head with my hockey stick. There was a crack and then a thud when his head hit the floor. After that, he didn't move a muscle so I grabbed my gear and legged it.'

'Bloody hell!'

'And now it seems the police are trying to frame Miss Evans. She discovered the body and might've left some fingerprints or something. I don't see how they can have any real evidence against her but, these days, people are forced to sign false confessions. You read about it in the papers all the time.'

'I wouldn't put anything past the pigs!' Phillips

fumed. He paused, 'But a hockey stick! Couldn't you have settled for a punch? We've all wanted to do that.'

'You don't understand!' David protested. 'I had no choice. He might've looked fat and unfit, but it was the only way I could stop him raping me.'

'Oh, come on,' Phillips spluttered, his mouth gaping in disbelief.

David's face flushed with emotion and his blue eyes seemed to darken. 'It's the truth, I swear! That bastard had been fucking me for two years, and I couldn't take it any longer. I warned him to stay away but, when I threatened him with the stick, he just laughed in my face. He kept coming, like he'd done so many times before. He was sure I didn't have the guts to protect myself, but I pole-axed the bugger with one blow, like David and Goliath. I couldn't believe how easy it was.'

'Why the hell didn't you tell someone earlier?' an appalled Phillips asked.

'Remember, Ed, I was thirteen when he started groping me. I was smaller then, and his sweaty hands and body were much stronger than mine. He was powerful and frightening. When I said I'd tell my parents, he went berserk. He even threatened to harm my mother. After he'd been up my arse a few times, I suppose he felt safe to carry on. When he'd finished, he would go on about how sorry he was for losing control of himself. If I wasn't so handsome, he'd say, nothing would've happened – as if it was all my fault! Or he'd insist I was queer and enjoyed what he did. But he always reminded me that, if I ever told anyone, it'd be his word against mine, and nobody would believe a schoolboy over a Headmaster, especially one who wore a dog collar. Until now, I've never mentioned any of this to a living soul, though I'd arranged to meet Miss Evans to tell her about it last Sunday.'

'Well, you mustn't keep quiet any longer,' hissed an indignant Phillips. 'What you did wasn't murder, it was self-defence. That evil bastard deserved everything he got. In the old days, they slaughtered the surplus animals in November. Blood Month, they called it. That's all you did. You rid the world of a useless beast. People will thank you for it. No jury in the land will convict you of anything, so don't worry on that score. But it's time you told your parents. Get them to take you to the police and sort out this mess. When you tell them what Griffiths was up to, they won't lock you up. They'll probably recommend you for a bloody medal!'

A sigh of relief escaped from David's lips. 'I hadn't looked at it that way. You've made me feel more hopeful, but I'm not sure I can face telling my mother such horrible things.'

'If I were you, I'd be more worried about your father. Decent men can react violently when someone harms their kid. Your mum might well be the calmer one. How about telling Mr Thomas first? The old cynic believes the worst of everyone, and he couldn't stand Griffiths. I'll come with you, if you like. Let him contact your parents. If they're summoned to school, they'll be expecting bad news. It's the only way to get the police to release Miss Evans. And that's what you want, isn't it?'

'All right, Ed, you've convinced me. Let's do it, before I chicken out.'

13

17th November

Rhian woke with a start and a shiver and began to tremble. Her legs were almost devoid of sensation so she bunched her knees into her chest to conserve body heat. Huddled in a ball like a hedgehog, she shivered under a single blanket and stared at the painted brick wall of the police cell. She had emerged from a fretful sleep but, inside her skull, could still hear the word 'murderer' tolling.

She raised her wrist to look for the time only to recall that her watch had been confiscated hours ago. Thunderbolts shot through her head and a wave of nausea began to stir in her stomach. Suddenly, there was a stinking mess on the floor. She propped herself on one elbow, experiencing no relief from her misery.

A key rattled in the lock and the florid face of the Duty Sergeant appeared round the door. 'Been having a nightmare, have we? You've woken the whole bloody nick with your screaming and shouting, and I see you've made a pigsty of the place too. Well, you'll have to wallow in it till the morning because I'm not cleaning it up,' he sneered.

With a slam of the metal door, he plunged Rhian into

depths of unfathomable loneliness. Ridiculously, she was embarrassed by her inability to control her outpourings, so determined to stay awake to avoid another outburst.

'She's proving more stubborn that I expected,' Jones said later, 'but Sergeant Harris says she cried herself to sleep last night and 'as puked all over the place. He reckons she'll crack before long. Another few hours might do the trick.'

'Good. Let's see how she reacts to the prospect of a lifetime in a cell. She can count herself lucky. Not so long ago, she'd be facing the hangman for what she's done. I need to get a confession before some solicitor advises her to shut up. Whether she coughs or not, I intend to charge her with murder.' Determination glinted in Llewellyn's dark, hooded eyes.

Their conversation was interrupted by a fresh-faced constable who looked too immature to grow stubble. 'Excuse me, sir.'

'Yes, what is it? I'm busy.'

'It's about the Griffiths' case. There's a lad downstairs who claims he's the murderer.'

The detectives stared at each other. For a moment, the garrulous duo were struck dumb.

Then Jones muttered, 'It's bound to be a nutcase or some sad bugger who can't get any attention other than by wasting police time. I'll soon get rid of 'im.'

14

17th November

Apart from cadavers in the mortuary, Llewellyn had never seen a face so deathly as that of the golden-haired youth who sat before him. It was obvious that the boy was under considerable stress and unlikely to be an attention seeker, but the detective's faith in his gut reaction was powerful. He was convinced he knew the murderer's identity and would be loath to accept any other confession.

The youth exuded the air of a shell-shock victim, so Llewellyn simply asked for an account of what had happened in the school's changing room on the afternoon in question. If he was a liar, it should prove easy enough to catch him out.

David told his sordid tale slowly and thoughtfully, trying not to forget any details. He had almost grown accustomed to relating it. After Edward Phillips had come a surprisingly sympathetic Mr Thomas, and then, worst of all, his parents. His mother had wept a little but his father – normally a calm, rational scientist – had erupted with a fury which upset his son so much that David had briefly regretted his decision to confess. Eventually, the storm of indignation passed and common sense had reasserted itself. The decision to go to the police had been taken, and not only for Miss Evans' sake.

Tom Llewellyn did not interrupt the youth's narrative until he described his assault upon the Reverend Griffiths, and the reason for it.

'So you told the Headmaster that, if he tried to force himself upon you again, you'd resort to violence. Is that what you're saying?'

'Yes. I was clutching my stick in both hands and I warned him not to come any closer or I'd use it. But he just laughed. Then he lunged at me. I swung the stick and caught him on the forehead. It was like switching a light out. The sound of his head thudding on the floor made me physically sick.'

'We found no vomit anywhere,' Llewellyn objected.

'I managed to reach the toilets.'

'What did you do next?'

David's blue eyes became watery. 'If he'd shown any signs of life, I'd have called for help because I never meant to kill him. All I wanted was to stop him raping me. That's the truth!'

Llewellyn continued in a softer tone. 'A few more questions and then you can go home. How do you know the Headmaster was dead? Did you check whether he was breathing or had a pulse?'

'No, nothing like that. I was sure he was dead because he didn't make a sound or move a muscle.'

'And then?'

'I grabbed my stuff and ran for it. I didn't stop till I got home.'

'Where's your stick now?'

'In my bedroom.' He added, in a whisper, 'But I've wiped it clean.'

'We'll still need to have it examined. Go round and pick it up, Sergeant,' Llewellyn ordered, and Jones made a reluctant exit. 'Did anyone see you when you came out of the changing room?'

'I don't think so. I saw Miss Morris, but she was putting some rubbish into the bins outside the kitchen. If she'd seen me running, she'd have told me off. She's like that.'

'So you thought you'd got away with it, eh?' the detective mused provocatively.

'I knew I'd done a terrible thing and wanted to get as far from there as possible. If the Headmaster had listened to me, he'd still be alive.'

'Point taken, but why did you only decide to come forward and confess when you heard that Miss Evans might be charged with murder?'

'Because I knew she was innocent.'

'Is that the only reason?'

David gave the detective a quizzical look but replied firmly, 'Yes.'

'You see, shortly before the Headmaster's murder,

superior's assertion. 'The boy has confessed and you've just said he's honest!'

Llewellyn took two draws on the pipe and a sip of beer and grinned. 'Think back to the pathologist's report, Jack. We know that Griffiths was knocked out in the changing room. But then he was dragged into the showers and held down to drown. Where we went wrong was to assume that both deeds were committed by the same person. They weren't. David thinks he killed Griffiths, but we know better. He assaulted the Headmaster and left him unconscious on the floor. Not dead. In the course of our interview, he never mentioned touching the body, let alone moving it. So someone else must have finished him off. My money is still on Evans. The motive is unaltered. If anything, I think the case against her is stronger than ever.

'Imagine how the Headmaster must've felt when he received that letter. One of his staff was accused of fancying the very pupil he'd been abusing for the past two years! Suddenly, an attractive young woman was a potential rival for the boy and a dangerous one at that. David might tell her about what he was doing to him. Evans had to go, and thanks to the contents of that letter, it was easy enough to engineer her dismissal.

'A few hours later, the Headmaster lay senseless on the floor in the sports pavilion. What if it was Evans who stumbled upon him? Remember that Griffiths was about to wreck her career. What would you have done? Even a saint would've been tempted to finish him off.

The Headmaster's death would allow her to remain in teaching. Then, all she had to do was remove the incriminating evidence in the letter and keep her fingers crossed that he'd not told anyone about it.'

Jones whistled softly to show he was impressed. 'So you reckon Evans stole the letter.'

'No-one else had reason to take it. We still have a motive and the opportunity for murder, and Evans has no alibi. A confession will be the icing on the cake.'

'What's going to happen to the boy?'

'He'll have to be medically examined and perhaps given some counselling, but I've no intention of taking any action against him. He needs help, not punishment, for what's happened.'

'Will we charge Evans in the morning?'

'Before we do, I want you to visit Miss Morris for a chat. The lad said she was the only person he saw when he was running away from the crime scene. Evans is adamant that she didn't leave the boarding house between three and five o'clock last Saturday afternoon. If Miss Morris saw her in the vicinity of the changing rooms between those times, it'll be the final nail in her coffin.'

16

18th November

Darkness had begun to creep around her Victorian cottage as Janet Morris put on a record of the adagietto from Mahler's *Fifth Symphony* to match her mood. Days of tears and unspoken despair had taken their toll. She sat and stared at the silhouette of a Scots pine which stood at the end of her garden. Above its blackness was a smear of ochre. The wind had dropped and the air was still, auguring a frost. As the last glimmerings submitted to night, her reverie was shattered by two crashes of the brass door knocker.

'I'm sorry to disturb you, Miss Morris,' Jones apologised, 'but can I 'ave a word? It won't take long.'

'That's quite all right, Sergeant. To be honest, I could do with the company. Would you like a cup of tea? I was about to put the kettle on.'

'Oh, that's very civil of you.'

As the nut-brown liquid gurgled into a cup, Jones asked Miss Morris to cast her mind back to the previous Saturday afternoon. 'I gather you usually help out with the teas after matches.'

'That's right. I lay tables, cut sandwiches, make tea, that sort of thing. Afterwards, I help with the washing-up. When Mr Davies was Headmaster, his wife supervised the catering staff but, as John was a bachelor, I offered my services.'

'Would I be correct in assuming you 'ad a high opinion of the Reverend Griffiths?'

'Oh, yes indeed. He was a God-fearing man, a strict but fair disciplinarian and an excellent leader. His death will deal a terrible blow to the school's fortunes.'

Her earnestness persuaded Jones not to destroy her illusions just yet. 'Time will tell, but one of your pupils 'as been down to the station to report an altercation he had with the Reverend Griffiths in the sports pavilion after last Saturday's hockey match.'

'One of our boys? No, I can't believe it!' she protested.

'Well, his story fits the facts like a glove, and he comes across as a plausible young man.'

'Who is he?' Miss Morris snapped. 'I'll tell you whether you can trust him.'

'I'd rather not reveal his identity, but he mentioned that he saw you as he was running away.'

'Me?'

'He says you were putting some rubbish into the dustbins at the rear of the kitchen so he only saw your back but, if you could confirm his story, it would help us. Do you remember catching sight of anyone hurrying from the changing rooms?'

Miss Morris frowned. 'No, I don't. You're not suggesting that one of our boys was responsible for John's death, are you?'

'We don't think he actually killed the Headmaster.'

'Thank the Lord!' she gasped. 'Think of the publicity that would cause. It's been horrible enough already. We can't afford to lose any more pupils.'

You don't know the half of it, Jones thought, but he merely asked, 'Did you see anyone else in the vicinity? A member of staff perhaps?'

'I really can't recall seeing anybody, Sergeant. It was almost dark by then. There's a light above the kitchen door which is probably why the boy noticed me. Now I come to think of it, Margaret Harrold was washing some dishes about that time. You get a good view of the sports pavilion from the kitchen window, so she might have seen him, I suppose.'

'Right then, I'll pay Mrs Harrold a quick visit just in case. Are those Welsh cakes homemade?'

17

18th November

Jones' nose wrinkled upon contact with the stale air of the senior boarding house. The aroma of sweaty feet was unmistakable. He pressed the bell to the Harrolds' flat and waited. Eventually, the door was opened by a harassed-looking woman with unkempt hair.

'Can I help you?' she asked, failing to recognise the visitor.

Jones displayed his warrant card and introduced himself. 'I'm sorry to disturb you this late in the day, but I'd be obliged if you'd answer a couple of questions in connection with the Reverend Griffiths' death. I've just driven over from Miss Morris' home. It was, more or less, her suggestion that I speak to you.'

'What on earth is the woman thinking?' Mrs Harrold cried.

Jones thought she looked and sounded oddly alarmed.

'I made it clear to the officer who interviewed me last weekend that the Headmaster's death is a mystery to me. I don't see how I can help you.'

Aware of a group of eavesdropping pupils along the corridor, Jones made his request more forcefully. 'If you'd prefer to answer my questions at the station, Mrs Harrold, that's fine by me.'

'There's no need to adopt that tone, Sergeant,' she retorted. 'Of course you may come in, and I'll do my best to assist your enquiries, but you're wasting your time.'

Dr Harrold was seated in an armchair by a coal fire which glowed in a cast-iron grate. He was watching the news on a portable television. Unlike his wife, he looked comfortable, but his face registered consternation when the detective entered.

'This police officer wishes to speak to me, dear. Apparently, Janet Morris thinks I may be able to help with his enquiries. I can't imagine why.'

'It's not the most convenient of times,' said Dr Harrold, as he got to his feet and switched off the set.

Jones sighed. 'I've already apologised to your wife, sir. I wouldn't disturb you without good cause. I take it you're as keen to lay this matter to rest as we are.' There was something about this supercilious pair which made it difficult to be polite.

'That goes without saying. Do you want me to leave the room?'

'There's no need for that.' Jones turned to look at Mrs Harrold but she avoided eye contact by staring over his shoulder at her husband. 'All I want to know is whether you saw anyone coming from the sports pavilion about twenty minutes after the finish of the hockey match last Saturday.'

Without a moment's hesitation, she replied, 'No, I didn't.'

'According to Miss Morris,' Jones persisted, 'you were washing some dishes in the kitchen at that time, so you had a clear view of the doorway. It might help us if you could recall seeing anyone in the vicinity.'

Mrs Harrold made no pretence at racking her memory before insisting, 'I saw nobody. I'm certain of it. Anyway, it was dark by then.'

'But the doorway was well lit,' Jones said. 'What about the Headmaster?'

'Oh, for God's sake!' she snapped. 'How many more times? I was too busy to notice anyone.'

Jones scratched his bald head slowly, as if to try and collect his thoughts. 'That's that, then. It was a long shot but, in a murder enquiry, we have to follow up every lead.'

'I'll show you to the door, Sergeant,' Dr Harrold intervened.

'Unfortunately, sir, there've been some developments in our investigation which might 'ave quite an impact on the school. Now you're acting Headmaster, I'll bring you up-to-date while I'm 'ere. Perhaps I could 'ave a word in private?'

'We can talk in my study,' said Dr Harrold, shooting a nervous glance at his wife.

As he ensconced himself behind a desk which occupied most of the floor space in the book-lined room, Dr

Harrold said, 'Sit down, Sergeant. Now what's this news that you're being so secretive about?'

The acting Headmaster was tapping the tips of his fingers together, a habit which Jones found irritating. He also noticed that all of the books were meticulously ordered according to height which only served to increase his dislike of this bumptious man.

'We've reason to believe that two people were involved in the murder, though we think they were acting separately.'

Dr Harrold frowned. 'I don't follow your meaning.'

'Well, sir, it's likely that the Headmaster was knocked out by one person and then drowned by somebody else. One of your pupils 'as admitted to being involved.'

'Dear God!' gasped Dr Harrold. 'Are you sure? John Griffiths may have been in his fifties, but he was a powerful fellow. I doubt if any of our pupils would be capable of rendering him unconscious.'

'The lad 'it him with his hockey stick.'

'His hockey stick? Really, Sergeant, this is bordering on the ludicrous.'

'I 'aven't come to the bizarre bit yet,' Jones replied, now keen to wipe the smirk from Harrold's face. 'The boy was having to defend himself because your colleague had been sexually assaulting him for two years.'

Dr Harrold looked at Jones aghast. 'Don't be absurd!' The shocked expression on his skinny face seemed genuine even to Jones' jaundiced eye. 'You must be aware that it's not unknown for pupils to invent outlandish stories as a means of gaining revenge upon teachers who've punished them. And a dead man is in no position to defend himself.'

'True,' Jones agreed reluctantly.

'So, Sergeant, I would advise you to be wary of accepting this boy's allegations at face value. If such rumours were to become public, they would create havoc with the school's reputation.'

'I realise that, sir, which is why I cautioned you about the need for discretion. But what matters is whether the lad 'as told the truth or not. Have any teachers or parents expressed concern about Griffiths? After all, he was a middle-aged bachelor working in a boys' boarding school. Did you never suspect him of such tendencies?'

'What I do know is that the Headmaster spent a lot of time in Janet Morris's company and there was speculation about marriage. Hardly the behaviour of a pederast! I didn't know the man very well, I didn't care for his company, and he was a hopeless Headmaster, but I really don't think he would have harmed a pupil in that way.'

A puzzled frown creased Jones' face. In spite of all his learning, Dr Harrold seemed extraordinarily ignorant about human nature. The detective also knew that he might as well try to command the waves as try to convince such a stubborn man about the futility of his opinions so he changed tack. 'How did you feel about Griffiths' appointment, sir?'

'I was stunned rather than angry. Several governors had assured me that the job was mine and the interviews were a formality. Of course, when Commander Hopkin announced his name, I wasn't aware that both men were Freemasons. My handshake, it seems, caused my downfall.'

Jones sympathised. 'It'd only be human to resent taking orders from someone you didn't respect. I'd 'ave harboured a grudge against him myself.'

Dr Harrold considered this for a moment, and then shook his head. 'That would have done no good. I got on with my work and did it as well as I could. It wasn't always easy, but that's history now. Whatever our differences, I wouldn't want the late Headmaster's reputation besmirched.'

'Fair enough. I suppose you'll get the job on a permanent basis now,' Jones speculated.

'Let's say that I'm not taking anything for granted, but I'm hoping the governors will favour an internal appointment on this occasion.'

'Better the devil you know, eh? Remind me where you were at half-past four last Saturday, sir.'

'Seated at this desk, Sergeant. I was correcting essays, the bane of a schoolmaster's life.'

18

21st November

Tom Llewellyn lived in an isolated cottage in the Vale of Glamorgan. On one side of his home was a tumble-down stable which served as a shed and garage and, on the other, was an ivy-clad copse where a few crows nested.

The cottage had been in need of modernisation when he had bought it in 1962. It still was. Somehow, he had never found the time, or inclination, to install the modern necessities of a damp-proof course, central heating and double glazing. He had changed the colour of the paint on the walls, and then covered them with his own watercolour landscapes of the Brecon Beacons, but little else.

As the years slipped by, he had become increasingly fond of his surroundings. He enjoyed scouring the woodland for fallen branches to saw into fuel for his beloved log fires. He liked peering through the leaded lights on misty mornings. Only when he was obliged to scrape frost from the inside of his bedroom windows did he sometimes regret his neglect. There was little incentive to transform his draughty den without someone to share it. Since his fiancée had left him – to marry his best friend – in his early thirties, domestic matters, like his sex life, had taken second place to his career.

During the night, winter had launched its first offensive and two inches of snow lay on the ground. Llewellyn, comfortable as a cat before the crackling fire, gazed in awe at nature's skilful softening of the stark November woods. Once the snow relented, he would venture into the silent stillness and try to capture its spirit in his own simple style.

Suddenly, a face, masked by a balaclava, appeared at the window! A pair of dark eyes were boring into him. His heart skidded through several beats.

'What the hell!' he shouted, leaping from the leather armchair. Plenty of villains had cause to seek revenge for what he had done to them in the past. The intruder's knuckles began to beat a tattoo on the glass and a finger pointed ominously towards the front door. Then the mask was peeled away revealing a shiny dome.

Llewellyn rushed to the door and greeted Jones with a flurry of expletives. 'Why are you wearing one of those bloody things? You could've given me a heart attack!'

'Sorry, sir,' Jones apologised. 'I didn't think about how I looked. It's no joke 'aving snow melt on your pate, you know. This is my eldest boy's. It's great. My 'ead's warm as toast. And I did ring your bell several times, but it still doesn't work. I told you it needed fixing the last time I came.'

'Some of us have better things to do than repair doorbells. Now you'd better have a good excuse for coming here on a Sunday. Take a seat. No, not the one by the fire. That's mine.'

'It's about the Evans woman, sir. I'm not sure she's our murderer, after all.'

Llewellyn gave a long sigh of exasperation. 'We've been through all this, Jack. I've never charged an innocent person with murder in my career. Evans is guilty as sin and she'll be remanded in custody by the magistrates tomorrow.'

Jones' crestfallen face caused him to continue, 'Come on, then, let's hear it. What's happened to change your mind?'

His sergeant did not need asking twice. 'If Evans is guilty, I reckon we'd 'ave cracked her by now. My chat with the Harrolds has made me think along a different track. It strikes me that Dr Harrold also 'ad a motive and the opportunity for murdering Griffiths. What's more, I got the feeling that he and his wife were lying through their teeth when I spoke to them. For someone who claimed to 'ave seen nothing, Mrs Harrold's reaction to my questions bordered on hysteria.'

'Go on,' Llewellyn said, when Jones paused for breath.

'Well, Mrs Harrold admits she was washing dishes in the school kitchen at about the time of the murder and that she could see the pavilion doorway which, as you know, was well lit. Yet she says she noticed nobody go in or out.'

'Hardly surprising, if she was up to her elbows in soapsuds,' interjected his superior.

'But what if she saw someone who she'd want to protect? What if she saw her husband?'

'You've no evidence to support this theory, I presume?'

'About as much as you've got against Evans,' Jones retorted. 'Let's be 'onest, sir, the lab boys have come up with bugger all. Unless you get her to confess, you 'aven't a hope of getting a murder charge to stick.'

'Come off it, Jack!' Llewellyn replied indignantly. 'A witness linking her to the scene of crime would make me more confident, but Commander Hopkin is ready to testify that Griffiths told Evans that he was about to destroy her career and reputation only hours before his murder. Now that's what I call a motive! Any jury is bound to find the disappearance of Lewis's incriminating letter very suspicious. Remember that Evans was one of only a handful of people who knew of its existence. Why would anyone else take it? And even a half-competent barrister will make something of the fact that she just happened to be the one who found the body. Evans had good reason to kill. What's Dr Harrold's motive?'

'He didn't dislike Griffiths, sir, he couldn't stand the sight of 'im. He resented being passed over for a man he considered his inferior and, on qualifications and experience, he was the better man for the job.'

'If I'd bumped off every idiot who's beaten me to promotion over the years, I'd be a serial killer myself,' Llewellyn chuckled. 'No, it won't do.'

'But their feud was wrecking the Harrolds' marriage, sir! Everyone says they were a happy couple till Griffiths turned up. According to Arthur Thomas, since Harrold failed to get the top job, he's hit the booze in a big way and this was causing trouble at home. Rumours of divorce had begun to fly about.

'So, what if it was Harrold who chanced upon the Headmaster when he was out for the count? Nothing premeditated. The man he despised was lying at his feet. No witnesses around. It would take a couple of minutes to finish him off. Then the job he craved would be 'is, and he'd be able to save his marriage into the bargain. It was the chance of a lifetime and I reckon he took it.'

'And his wife's nerves are in a mess because she's having to cover for him, eh?'

'Well, that's what I think. Miss Morris put me on to her. She told me about Mrs Harrold being in the kitchen at the time of the assault. I checked it out and, from the sink, you get a perfect view of the pavilion entrance. She even mentioned that Mrs Harrold had disappeared without finishing the dishes, which was most unlike her.'

'So?'

'If she'd seen her husband, gone out to speak to him, and discovered what he'd done, she wouldn't 'ave gone back into the kitchen. They probably rushed off home and concocted the tale that he'd been marking books all afternoon while she'd been helping with the teas.'

'Mm,' mused Llewellyn. 'It's plausible, I suppose.' He lit his pipe and puffed thoughtfully on it. 'But, then again, if I can get Mrs Harrold to say she saw Evans coming out of the sports pavilion, I'd be home and dry. No, she's staying under lock and key.'

Jones dug in his wallet and pulled out a note. 'I've a fiver 'ere which says Harrold is the murderer.'

'I'll happily take your cash, Jack. We've got the culprit already. But, in the morning, we'll pay the Harrolds a surprise visit and try a little bluff on them. It'll be interesting to watch their reaction.'

'Thank you, sir. Now I'd better be making a move. If I'm late for Sunday lunch, I get an ear bashing from the missus as it's the only family meal we get nowadays. And the boys want me to help them build a snowman this afternoon.'

'Be quick then,' said Llewellyn, pointing to a newly sunlit sky, 'because it's thawing fast.' He brushed some tobacco ash from his trousers. His face looked rather wistful when he added, 'I sometimes wish I'd had children.'

Jones laughed. 'Forty-five isn't too late to start a family.'

'Forty-four, actually.'

The midday sunshine was causing rivulets of melting snow to rush down the cottage's Welsh slate roof. As he gave the departing Jones a farewell wave, a clump of flakes fell from a treetop and slithered, unwelcome as a snake, down Llewellyn's neck.

19

22nd November

Nothing remained of Sunday's snow. A few clouds scudded past the school's clock tower as it struck eight o'clock. The detectives were surprised to see a few boys already wandering about.

Llewellyn hoped to catch Dr Harrold at breakfast, something guaranteed to irritate the most placid of souls. He wanted to goad him into saying something indiscreet, if not incriminating. Once they were at the station, there was less chance of inducing a slip of the tongue.

Jones pressed the Harrolds' bell. The door opened to reveal a mousy-looking woman who, by the expression on her face, regarded their arrival with alarm. 'Not again,' she moaned. 'Why can't you leave us alone? We've already told you all we know.' Her voice began to rise in pitch and volume. 'We've nothing more to say. For God's sake, leave us in peace!' With that, she slammed the door.

Jones smiled, raised a thumb, and left it on the bell until the door was reopened. Though anger inflamed Dr Harrold's face, he was straining to retain control of his temper. 'Come in gentlemen. I don't want any unseemly scenes in front of the boys.'

Llewellyn was pleased. Their timing was perfect. On the small dining table, a half-eaten boiled egg was going cold and a copy of the *Daily Telegraph* was propped against a jar of marmalade.

'I must protest about this invasion of our privacy at such an hour, Chief Inspector. When we spoke to Sergeant Jones recently, we emphasised that we had nothing to add to our original statements. My wife and I are beginning to feel harassed. I think a complaint about your intrusions may be in order.'

'You did invite us in, sir,' Llewellyn replied coldly.

'Well, what do you want?'

'As acting Headmaster, I thought you should be the first to know that I intend releasing Miss Evans from custody today as I'm now convinced that she can't assist our enquiries any further. She can resume her teaching duties whenever you like.' Llewellyn lied so convincingly that even Jones was inclined to believe him.

Dr Harrold's face blanched. 'I don't understand. I was under the impression that you thought she was involved in the murder.'

'Whatever gave you that idea, sir?' Jones asked, an impish grin crossing his face.

'We've no intention of bringing charges against Miss Evans,' Llewellyn broke in. 'From the information she, another member of staff, and one of your pupils have provided, I now believe I know the identity of the Headmaster's murderer.'

'Then who is it?' asked Dr Harrold bluntly, as he and his wife exchanged a glance that, to Llewellyn's experienced eye, seemed to convey sheer horror.

The detective laughed. 'Oh, I'm not at liberty to divulge that sort of information, sir.' Then, in a more sombre tone, he continued, 'Let's just say that I'd be obliged if you would accompany me to the station to answer some questions. I assume you'd have no objection to Detective Sergeant Jones staying here with your wife to take a look around. Perhaps you should inform Miss Morris of your whereabouts as you could well be absent from your duties for some time.' Llewellyn was doing his utmost to conjure the clanking of tumbrel wheels in every syllable he uttered.

'I hope you're not implying that I had anything to do with the Headmaster's death!' Dr Harrold gasped.

'You can infer what you like, but we're going to Bridgend to continue this conversation on a more formal basis.'

As he said these words, Llewellyn made a slight movement towards Dr Harrold which caused his wife, who had been silent throughout these exchanges, to leap to her husband's defence by jumping between them.

'Don't touch him!' she shouted. 'He had nothing to do with it! I did it! I killed the Headmaster!' Mrs Harrold turned to her husband and was enveloped in his arms. She began to weep, her breath coming in ragged gasps.

The detective duo stared at each other bemused.

Jones put a hand to his eyes and rubbed them as if to assure himself that he was not dreaming. This was not the outcome either of them had been anticipating.

For a few moments Mrs Harrold was allowed to regain control of her emotions. When her sobs subsided, Llewellyn asked, 'How did you kill him?'

'Don't say anything, dear,' Dr Harrold pleaded, in vain.

'It's too late now. If I get this off my chest, perhaps I'll be able to sleep again.' She paused and then explained, 'I thought it strange when I noticed the Headmaster go into the changing rooms after everyone else had left for tea. Then, a few minutes later, when Janet Morris was outside, I saw a boy come rushing out...'

'David Wyn-Williams?'

'That's right. I got the impression he'd been up to no good and didn't want to be spotted. Janet had her back to him, and she's a bit deaf so didn't notice him, but I thought there was something suspicious about his behaviour. I decided to go and take a look around. I thought I'd find a broken window or some graffiti...'

'But you found the Headmaster unconscious on the floor,' Jones interjected again, to his superior's irritation.

'Yes, Sergeant, he was lying in a crumpled heap. I could hardly believe my eyes. My first thought was that he'd had a heart attack but, when I went closer, it was obvious he'd been struck across the forehead. I was hoping he was dead, but I felt his breath touch my hand. There and then, I made up my mind to finish him off.'

Mrs Harrold paused to wipe a tear from her eye. Her husband put his arm around her neck and she resumed. 'I don't know where the strength to drag him into the showers came from. I pushed his face into the drainage trough, turned the stopcock on and pressed my hands on the back of his head. It didn't take very long. The truth is I felt no more pity for him than if I'd been drowning an unwanted animal. Then I came back here and changed my wet clothes. That's all there was to it.'

Llewellyn asked, 'Did you notice if David was carrying anything?'

Mrs Harrold considered the question carefully before replying.

'Yes, I think he had a bag in one hand and a hockey stick in the other.'

'Was it Wyn-Williams who knocked the Headmaster unconscious?' Dr Harrold asked.

'Yes, it was,' Llewellyn replied. 'I don't know if it's of any consolation, but the Headmaster had been abusing David sexually for a long time. The boy struck him in self-defence.'

'Griffiths'll be burning in 'ell as we speak,' Jones added.

Llewellyn shook his head at this metaphysical speculation but Mrs Harrold managed a feeble smile and said, 'My husband told me about those allegations after your last visit, Sergeant. He tried to convince me that they justified what I'd done but, of course, they didn't.'

'So your husband knew all about it from the beginning?' Llewellyn asked in the confiding tone which both policemen had now adopted.

Margaret Harrold suddenly grasped the implications of his question and protested, 'It was all my doing! I don't want Derek involved!'

'We'll make a clean breast of things together, dear,' Dr Harrold intervened. 'I was marking essays when I heard Margaret return earlier than expected. When I saw the sodden state of her clothes and she told me what had happened, I was horrified, but also determined that she wasn't going to spend her life in prison for removing a stain on humanity like Griffiths. Since then, she's hardly slept a wink but, when you took Miss Evans into custody, Margaret became much more agitated. If you'd charged an innocent woman with murder, I think my wife would've confessed, despite my feelings on the subject. You look sceptical, Chief Inspector, but it's true. Margaret's Christian faith runs much deeper than mine. Coping with the guilt was crushing her.'

Llewellyn denied the accusation. 'Actually, sir, I do believe you.'

'What you can't understand is the damage that man inflicted upon our marriage,' Mrs Harrold continued. 'He left Derek to run the school while he swanned around at meetings and dinners, taking the credit.

Over the past few years, I've had to watch my husband become a morose, short-tempered man. But what I found unbearable was that he turned to whisky for solace, rather than to me.'

She paused and stared at her husband before adding, 'I'm sorry, darling, but it's the truth. And it was all that bloody hypocrite's fault! I begged Derek to move back to London. I even threatened him with divorce, but he had his heart set on being Headmaster here. God knows why! That odious man Griffiths was destroying my life and I despised him. I only wish I'd known about what he was doing to Wyn-Williams because I'd have relished informing you about it. Nothing would have given me greater pleasure.'

Mrs Harrold's tirade subsided. Emptied of emotion, she sagged into her husband's embrace. He looked directly into Tom Llewellyn's dark eyes and said, 'I wouldn't want to live without Margaret. These events have brought us closer than ever. It may seem a dreadful thing to suggest, Chief Inspector, but that devil's death has probably saved our marriage.'

*

The detectives adjourned to the Red Lion for a liquid lunch to celebrate the outcome of the case. When asked what he would like to drink, Jones answered, 'As you don't owe me that fiver, sir, I'll have a small malt.'

'And mine's a pint of Brains bitter,' Llewellyn grunted at the barman.

'Cheers,' said Jones, as he knocked back the whisky in a single gulp. 'I reckon we can put that one down to luck rather than judgement. We nearly put Miss Evans away for life for something she didn't do and then, to make matters worse, we 'ad an innocent man lined up to take her place!' He shuddered. 'It doesn't bear thinking about.'

Llewellyn drew his chair closer to the log fire, took a sip of foaming ale which turned his moustache blond, and replied airily, 'Don't be too self-critical, Jack. Thanks to you, we were on the right track this morning, and my little bluff about releasing Evans worked far better than I dared hope. When all's said and done, what matters is that the guilty person will be going to gaol.'

'True, sir, but it wasn't the person either of us was expecting,' Jones retorted.

Llewellyn stared into the flickering flames and a twinkle appeared in his brown eyes as he said, 'Now don't quibble. The thing which irritates me is that I thought we were taking part in a murder mystery, not a bloody kitchen sink drama!'

20

22nd November

The depression which had besieged Rhian lifted the moment Llewellyn uttered the words, 'You're free to go, Miss Evans. We accept that you weren't involved in Griffiths' death and would like to apologise for detaining you so long.'

Rhian gave her captor a dismissive glance, but said nothing. She sensed that this was not the time nor place to launch a counteroffensive. That would come later with the aid of a solicitor. The past few days had wrought havoc with her life, and she would have her revenge.

'Mrs Harrold has made a full confession.'

'My God! I'd never have thought of her.'

'To be honest, it came as a bit of a shock to us too,' Jones admitted.

'If you'd like to come and get your belongings, I'll arrange for you to be driven back to Llanover Grange,' said Llewellyn. 'I expect you'll want a few days off to get over your ordeal but, as far as we're concerned, there's nothing to stop you teaching again, as soon as you feel up to it. Dr Harrold has been charged with a lesser offence, so I'm not sure who'll take over the running of the school. I rang Miss Morris earlier and told her what's happened. Of course, she was shocked by the news about the Harrolds, but she'll sort things out for you. She's been invaluable to us throughout this case.'

'She's living proof that nobody notices when the boss is away for a week but, if his secretary is absent for a day, all hell breaks loose,' Jones added.

The governors placed Llanover Grange in the safe hands of Arthur Thomas until the end of the Michaelmas Term. He was delighted with his elevation to such heights, even if only on a temporary basis. Taking advantage of his new status, he made strenuous efforts to persuade Rhian to continue their partnership beyond Christmas.

'I'm sorry, Arthur, but this school isn't for me. Griffiths was right. I'm not cut out for teaching.'

'Rubbish!' Mr Thomas snorted. 'You're a damn sight better than most of the chinless wonders we have here. You know your subject, you're good at communicating it and the boys like you. Anyway, what else can you do with a History degree?'

'I've decided to go home. My father owns a printing press and has always wanted me to go into the business and take it over when he retires. Perhaps I'll expand into publishing local history books. I'd enjoy that.'

Arthur Thomas lit a cigarette and dragged its noxious fumes deep into his lungs. Smoke snaked out of his nostrils as he conceded defeat. 'Well, if that's what you want, I shan't push you any further but remember, while I'm around, there'll be a place for you here. Just pick up the phone.'

'Thanks very much,' Rhian said, genuinely touched. 'But the person I feel sorry for is Janet Morris. When she discovers what a monster Griffiths really was underneath all that religious claptrap, she's going to get the shock of her life. I doubt if she'll ever trust a man again.'

'Well, you couldn't blame her. She's not got much to look forward to.'

'Now she'll be your secretary, Arthur, perhaps you should take her under your wing,' Rhian suggested. 'You've a few weeks to weave your charms.'

Her superior grinned as he fingered his thinning hair. 'That's an idea! Janet's a fusspot and always smells of coal tar soap, but she's not bad-looking, and she's a cracking cook. Spending retirement on my own doesn't appeal very much. I wonder if she likes the Gower? I've a cottage down there, you know.'

*

Miss Evans' reappearance in chapel caused stirrings of surprise. Arthur Thomas welcomed her return like that of a prodigal daughter and he instructed the Chaplain to proclaim her innocence from the pulpit.

Rhian scanned the waves of curious faces for David, but to no avail. It transpired that his parents had already removed him from Llanover Grange's malign clutches. The golden youth had transferred to a comprehensive school. Reality struck Rhian like a slap across the face.

21

29th November

It was almost midnight when the telephone in Saint Teilo's buzzed and interrupted Rhian's attempts at dozing off. She tried to ignore the droning but it persisted. Reluctantly, she swung herself out of bed. As she descended the stairs, her face wore a frown of foreboding because she knew from experience that late-night calls rarely brought good news.

She put the mouthpiece to her lips and strove to sound unconcerned. 'Hello.'

'It's Gareth,' he said, in a sheepish tone which confirmed her fears. 'I've been meaning to ring you to say sorry for the way things turned out.' In the weeks of separation, he had craved her body. He paused and then admitted, 'Since we broke up, I've been out with a couple of girls, but I've not slept with them. If you were to invite me round though, I wouldn't say no. A monk's life doesn't suit me.'

'You've been drinking,' she snapped.

'A few lagers! I'm not drunk, if that's what you mean. When I sent that letter, I never dreamt you'd become involved in a murder enquiry. The police must be stupid to hold someone like you for questioning. Any clown can tell you're not capable of murder.'

'Just of shagging schoolboys. Is that what you mean?'

His voice began to rise in volume. 'Well, let's face it, you did fancy that pretty boy. I'm broad-minded but...'

'You thought it OK to make allegations which were bound to wreck my career. The truth is you wanted revenge because I'd given you the elbow. You weren't interested in protecting my pupils. You wanted to hurt me. Simple as that.'

Stung by her sneering, Gareth's self-control evaporated. 'Bitch! You were a sad old virgin until I showed up. Everything you know about sex is what I taught you. And deny it all you like, but you were gagging for that boy!'

They traded insults until Rhian said, 'I'm pregnant.'

'You're what?'

'And you're the father.'

Gareth licked the salty droplets which broke on his upper lip. 'Are you sure it's mine?'

'I've never slept with anyone else. We're both at fault for not taking enough precautions. In future, you'd better be more careful as you're obviously capable of fathering children.'

Gareth realised that Rhian was in charge of events now. 'What are you going to do?'

'There's no way I'm becoming a single mother, so you

needn't worry on that score. One of your sperm isn't going to ruin my life.'

'Do you mean you're going to get rid of it?'

'My father has made the arrangements already. If you hadn't rung, I wouldn't have bothered telling you about it. Now I want you to know how much I've suffered by inviting you into my bed. It was the worst decision I've ever made.'

'Hang on! Don't I get a say in this? That kid is as much mine as yours.'

'Don't be ridiculous!' Rhian sneered. 'It's inside me! What you want is irrelevant. If I'd said I was keeping it, you'd be begging me to have an abortion.'

'Can we meet to talk about this?'

'No! I don't need a lecture on your rights. Everything's been arranged and I'm not backing out now.'

'Please…'

She slammed down the receiver and left him with the droning of the dialling tone.

Gareth did not move. In the span of a single phone call, he had gained, and lost, a child. Though Rhian's logic was hard to fault – marriage was out of the question and neither of them was equipped to raise a child alone – tears of frustration began to drip down his face.

22

17th December

The organ trumpeted, the choir launched into a descant and 'O Come All Ye Faithful' brought the Christmas service to a resounding close as it did every year. It was followed by the Headmaster's summary of the term's events and successes. As highlights were few, and disasters many, Mr Thomas kept his speech short, but he did not ignore Rhian's departure.

'Today,' he announced, 'we bid farewell to Miss Evans, our junior History teacher and my Assistant in Saint Teilo's. She's decided to take up a position outside teaching in Cardiff. In the brief time she's been with us, she has made a favourable impression, and I'd like to thank her for her service to the school. We wish her well in the future.' Shocked whispering greeted this announcement, which suggested the secrecy surrounding her departure had been well-maintained.

The rest of the morning passed in a flurry of tidying rooms and chasing lost books. A few leavers brought round autograph books for their friends and teachers to sign. After a turkey dinner, the reports were distributed. The Form Captain of 2B took Rhian unawares with a cry of 'Three cheers for Miss Evans!' which received a touchingly enthusiastic response. Then they were gone. Only a handful of boarders remained, idling away time until the family car drove into view.

Rhian emptied the contents of her desk. The deserted school was depressing. She hurried to Saint Teilo's to begin packing. There was no reason to delay her departure any longer. Her parents, who were saddened but realistic about their daughter's decision to end an unwanted pregnancy, declared her intention to join the family business as their best Christmas present ever.

Some clothes already nestled in a trunk when Edward Phillips poked his head around the half-open door. 'Excuse me, Miss, but I'll be pushing off soon and I wanted to say goodbye.'

'That's kind of you.'

'Actually, I've got something for you from the boarders. It's not much, but we didn't know you were going until this morning. During break, we had a whip-round and raised enough to buy this card and pen. It's a good one – a Parker – and I managed to get your name engraved on it. Mr Thomas gave me permission to go out and get it which was decent of him.'

'Yes, it was,' Rhian agreed. 'I didn't expect anything. It's not as if I've been here long. You'll thank the boarders for me next term, won't you?'

Phillips nodded as he handed her a monstrous pink envelope and a small gift-wrapped parcel. The interior of the card was plastered with good wishes and signatures scribbled in an assortment of garish colours. Rhian smiled at the messages but, before she could say anything, a couple of impatient notes sounded on a car horn.

'I'm wanted,' Phillips explained. He extended his hand and Rhian shook it warmly.

'Goodbye, Edward, and thanks.'

As he clattered down the stairs, Phillips shouted, 'And good luck, Miss!'

Swamped by a sable cloud of sadness, Rhian slumped into an armchair and watched the December sun die.

Epilogue

Nearly three years passed. Rhian was editing a badly written manuscript when a young man with long, honey-coloured hair and strikingly blue eyes entered her office. She looked up at him and blinked to make sure he was not a mirage. Then she smiled and said, 'I never expected to see you again. It's a lovely surprise. How did you find me?'

David laughed. 'It wasn't difficult. Edward Phillips told me you'd left to work in the family printing business in Cardiff. I looked in the directory and it only took a few phone calls. I'd have been disappointed if you'd not smiled when I came in. I've been wanting to speak to you for a long time, in fact, ever since you didn't turn up in the park on that awful Remembrance Day.'

'I wanted to be there!' Rhian interrupted. 'But I was answering endless police questions at the time. I was distraught at breaking my promise.'

'And I was frantic when you didn't appear. I waited ages so I could tell you about how Griffiths had been raping me. Of course, by then, I was convinced I'd killed him. I didn't know what the hell to do and I needed help. There was no-one else I trusted.'

Rhian was open-mouthed at this admission. 'Why me? We'd only spoken a couple of times.'

'Because you were in love with me…'

A vermillion flush swept across Rhian's face. 'How did you know that?'

'I think I knew it from the day you first laid eyes on me in chapel but, when I saw you staring into my bedroom from the bottom of our garden, I was sure of it. Teachers don't do that sort of thing. You must've realised I knew you were there, didn't you?'

Rhian saw no point in denying the truth. She had nothing to lose now. 'I suspected as much, but you didn't say a word when you came near, so I wasn't sure. If you'd shown any displeasure, I'd have stopped straight away.'

'Believe me, I looked forward to your visits. I was flattered that you found me attractive. Such open devotion from a teacher gave my confidence a much-needed boost. That's why I encouraged you so shamelessly. Stripping off like that! You must've thought I was a real poser!'

His candour and humour shocked and impressed her. How different he was from Gareth, she thought, but she still found his admission hard to believe. 'You're not having me on, are you?'

'No! You fancied me and I was trying to signal that I felt the same way, but I was too scared to say anything. Do you remember the day you took my class for Science? I virtually threw myself at you! When we were alone in the stockroom, I hoped you'd take the initiative and whisper something in my ear, but you didn't breathe a word, so I kept my mouth shut too.'

'My imagination – if not my tongue – was running riot, I can assure you. Teachers have to be so careful that it wasn't possible even to hint at my feelings.'

'A pity that bastard Griffiths didn't possess a fraction of your reticence,' David said. 'He was always going on about how much he adored me. Usually, after he'd been up my arse. When the police wanted to know if you'd ever shown any undue interest, I denied it instinctively. I didn't want them putting you into the same category as that old lecher. What I wanted never entered his head. With you, it was different.'

Rhian still looked dubious so he continued, 'When you came to watch me, I was excited. I enjoyed it. I wanted it. That's why I'm here today. I've not spoken to anyone else like this in my life but – somehow – I know we can trust each other.' He paused and a darkness entered his voice, 'Griffiths was vile. It's not just that he was fat and ugly and smelled of sweat. He was selfish and cruel. You don't rape someone you love. I meant no more to him than one of those blow-up dolls.'

A tear slid down Rhian's cheek so David crossed the room and enveloped her in a tender embrace. His scent and strength were thrilling. She recalled the futility of her attempts to make love to Gareth and whatever doubts she had entertained about David dissolved. He kissed her on the lips and she responded passionately.

When they separated, David said, 'My parents have always wanted me to go to university but I was never keen. Then I realised, if I came to Cardiff to study at the College of Music and Drama, I could do something I enjoyed, have the perfect excuse to live near you, and please my parents into the bargain. They know nothing about our feelings for each other and, as far as I'm concerned, what they don't know won't hurt them.'

Rhian smiled conspiratorially. 'For a while anyway.'

By the time David departed, the first link in an intimate and enduring relationship had been forged.

BOOKS BY WILLIAM VAUGHAN

The Midnight Ghost

A book for children about a Welsh chorister in a draconian boarding school who is bullied mercilessly until the ghost of a Benedictine novice steps out of the past to help him overcome his fears.

'The author has been bold to set the book within this exclusive community, but we gain a fascinating insight into this rather unique world, and the lessons learned about trust, friendship and bravery are timeless and universal. The story of Huw's developing maturity has pace and humour as well as ghostly intrigue and emotion. The dramatic climax is breath-taking.'

Hilary Cooper
(by permission of the Welsh Books Council)

The novel was chosen by the Welsh Books Council as one of the books to be used in its County Reading Competition for 2011–12.

The Black Legion

A book for young adults set during the French invasion of Pembrokeshire in 1797 which turns a short chapter in Welsh history into a vivid and gripping reality. Tom, a servant, and Megan, a Major's daughter, are caught up in dramatic events which will change their lives forever.

'A snappy swashbuckling adventure story that bristles with treachery and crackles with teenage love.'

Western Mail

Gold Hunter

A book for young adults set in Australia in the 1860s. A Welsh teenager sails from Cardiff to Adelaide in search of gold. He encounters drunkards, crocodiles, bushrangers and aboriginals and is then astonished to be offered half the profits in a gold mine. But, before his return to Llandaff, William Jenkins discovers that there are more important things in life than riches.

'This story has a whiff of the pioneering Wild West stories, is carefully written to draw the reader into the early days of the gold rush and explores an ever pertinent theme through an entertaining and exciting story. The character of William is particularly well-drawn...'

Janet Sim, from *School Librarian*

In the Welsh Icons Awards 2010, *Gold Hunter* was awarded runner up in the Children's Book of the Year category.